The

Daughter

Izzy James

The Dollmaker's Daughter
COPYRIGHT 2021 by Elizabeth C. Hull

Cover Art by *Nicola Martinez*
White Rose Publishing, a division of Pelican Ventures, LLC
www.pelicanbookgroup.com PO Box 1738 *Aztec, NM * 87410
White Rose Publishing Circle and Rosebud logo is a trademark of Pelican Ventures, LLC

Publishing History
First White Rose Edition, 2021
123456789
Electronic Edition ISBN 978-1-5223-0347-3
Paperback Edition ISBN 9781522303725
Published in the United States of America

Dedication

This one is for Caleb
"All you gotta do is..."

1

"Well, Miss Archer, it has been a long time," The grinning innkeeper bellowed loud enough to be heard in the yard. He rubbed his meaty hands together.

Amity cast quick glance into the main parlor. A cold rivulet slipped from her sodden cloak into her shoe. Yes, all the guests had taken note of his announcement of Amity's arrival. All went back to what they were doing when she caught their eye, except a tableful of men in hunting shirts dyed the same shade of indigo. They did not avert their gazes when she noticed them; rather she had the distinct impression she that they were assessing her as one might look over a new dog. An involuntary shiver ran down her shoulders.

Lucy, her maid, took a step closer.

Amity suppressed the chill, straightened her back, and turned to her host.

"Is your father with the carriage?" he asked.

"No, Mr. Burwell. My father was detained and will arrive tomorrow."

1

A puzzled look passed through his features before his smile returned. "Well, your rooms are ready." He waved a large hand toward a slender girl. "Mary, show Miss Archer to her room."

Amity said her thanks and followed Mary up a windowless flight of stairs to the second floor. Lucy followed them.

One dormer of six window lights cast watery shadows across a wooden framed bed. A cheery fire in the grate forced gloom into the corners of the small room.

"Mary, who are those men in the blue shirts in the chamber?"

Mary's blue eyes widened. "Shirtmen. They are riflemen come from Norfolk to protect us from the British."

Amity stiffened. "*They* are not here, are they?"

"The British? No, ma'am. The shirtmen just burned what was left of Norfolk. I heard them say they was waiting for orders."

"Thank you, Mary." Amity handed the girl a coin.

Mary bobbed a curtsey and left the room.

Amity shrugged out of her wet cloak to let the warmth melt her near frozen limbs. What she needed was a hot cup of coffee.

Lucy took Amity's cloak, a look of alarm in her large brown eyes. "Miss Amity, I don't like the looks them shirtmen was giving you down there. No one would mess with you if Mr. Reed was here."

Amity rolled her eyes. "We don't need Mr. Reed right now, what we need is a hot cup of coffee and something to eat."

Lucy huffed and turned to hang the cloak on a peg next to the door. She placed her own on the next peg.

A pang of guilt slashed through Amity. "I don't like the looks of those men either, hopefully they will leave soon. With my father and I here there cannot be room enough for all of them to stay."

Lucy's posture relaxed.

"And I am not leaving the ordinary. We will stay right here until Father comes. Except we have to go down to get something to eat. I could not possibly wait for them to carry up a tray. Are you not famished?"

Lucy nodded her agreement.

Amity's guilt assuaged, which left her empty stomach in charge.

They'd left immediately after breakfast. Twenty miles of frozen rain and mud ruts wore a body out. She needed to eat.

"Don'tcho be down there too long, Miss Amity."

"I will not. You go get something from the kitchen."

Amity peered out into the hallway before she stepped out of the room. Surely, no one would dare mess with her in a respectable establishment like Mr. Burwell's. While she'd shuddered at the innkeeper's announcement of her presence when she'd first arrived, it was precisely because she was known that she should feel safe. In fact, his little announcement might prove to be Providence at work.

Despite minor trepidation, giddiness shook her feet. So this was what it felt like to be out on one's own.

Throughout her twenty-five years, a sibling was always an elbow's distance away. She'd never spent the night alone away from home. Amity placed one gloved hand on the wall to keep from flying down the narrow staircase. Except for a thin rope of guilt yanking her back she could get quite used to this feeling of unfettered access to her wishes. The desire to wander and the guilt twined around each other deep in her soul. She couldn't explain the rambling temper. The guilt was more easily defined.

Her parents were good people. They'd always been kind and generous, some claimed overindulgent, with her and her siblings. How could she leave them to follow her own desires when the result would be stomach-aching worry over her? The inability to resolve the issue had left her stagnant. Waiting for she didn't know what.

Mr. Burwell met her at the foot of the stairs and showed her to a private parlor directly off the main room. Before long, a steaming cup of coffee and a plate of ham, fresh bread, and butter filled the table. Voices from the public chamber buzzed in the background.

This one night near Williamsburg on her own was almost too tempting. Her first opportunity to experience real life as it came. To fill her books with real happenings and real places instead of imaginings based on Lady Peabody's adventures in the courts of Europe and beyond. How far was it to the mountains? She had some money. The King's Highway would carry her a good bit of the distance in a carriage. Horseback from there. Assuming she could get a horse outside of Alexandria.

"Serve's 'em right. Tories the lot." A loud male voice floated into her reverie. "Burning's too good for 'em" The following general murmur seemed to agree with the outspoken man.

By her counting, it was the third time Norfolk had been burned. The first two happened before her brother, Field's, wedding on the sixth of January. Not that she'd been able to attend. Too dangerous to travel her mother said. According to her father, they were all to stay home for the duration of the war. Except for him, of course, he would travel to participate in the Committee. She stopped short of a thankful prayer for the commotion that had caused him to delay his departure. If the chariot had not been fully loaded, she may have had to wait for him to settle the disturbance with his foreman.

Well, it just showed that older people were over cautious. She'd made it almost to Williamsburg without any trouble whatsoever. She wasn't a schoolgirl after all; she'd recently turned twenty-five. And just when was she allowed to consider herself a woman?

"He just finished what he started, is all." A craggy voice rose above the others.

Amity craned her neck to see the speaker. What she saw was a sooty wall. Surely, it would be acceptable to step a little closer. She rose from her seat. If she were to improve her stories, she needed to see. Mr. Burwell would ensure her safety. She took step into the room and caught sight of a familiar shape approaching the door. *What is he doing here?*

Amity slid back out of the main chamber and into the far corner of her chair once Simon Morgan entered the ordinary. Her heart thudded against full lungs.

He glanced about the room before taking a seat facing away from where she sat in the deep shadow of age-darkened pine walls.

He could ruin everything. Well, she wasn't really running to the mountains anyway. Her mother would worry. Her father would blame himself. No. She would meet up with her father tomorrow and together they would travel to Aunty Clementine's exactly as planned.

But that didn't mean she had to endure Simon's company. If his usual ability to disregard the world while focusing on the book before him wasn't impaired by the laughter and conversation filling the tavern, she should be able to slip past him and make it up the stairs unnoticed.

Simon once again surveyed the full room after Mary took his order.

Amity willed herself to be invisible.

No doubt, her parents hoped she'd meet a suitable man in Williamsburg and settle down, but it wouldn't happen. She'd loved before and it came to naught. No. She would chronicle her travels. Once she gained a certain age, it wouldn't be scandalous. And why should it be? Master Phillips had made it clear that Virginia's manners were far less than he'd found in England. And so it should be. America would be a new nation free of nonsensical dictates. Amity would be an independent lady. A travel writer like Lady Peabody.

Amity pulled back once more when the door banged open to admit another young man. Boots scraped across the floor as he made his way to the bar. He ordered peach brandy.

From her seat, Amity could only glimpse his profile. Different from any man she'd ever seen, she couldn't take her eyes off him. He was tall, fine boned, dark hair pulled back in a queue, a hawk nose. He appeared loosely put together, not unlike Simon. Although Simon's looseness disarmed people, made them feel welcome. This man's fluidity recalled a cornered viper she'd seen in the barn at home—appropriating the space around him should he need to strike, or perhaps escape. A dark gaze captured her own.

Heat raced up her throat. Amity looked away quickly. When she dared to look up again he'd turned his back to her. "Good."

He seemed to be watching Simon and his dinner companion. Amity settled back into her chair. Perhaps she should stay a little bit longer. To say Simon misread people was an understatement. While it was an admirable quality to have never met a stranger, it was not always wise.

2

The smell of Norfolk burning stained the inside of Simon's nose. Throughout the wet ride toward Williamsburg, he couldn't escape the acrid fumes of the last of the buildings sacrificed in the name of independence. It was the right thing to do, but he couldn't help wondering what would happen to the people and the businesses they'd forged, some nearly a hundred years old.

Every part of his world swirled in turmoil. Hester insisted on staying with their aunt and uncle in Kemp's Landing instead of coming home with him to Maple Bridge where she would be safer. He couldn't find a way to like it, but Hester was a grown woman with a mind of her own. He couldn't control her any more than he could control Woodford and Howe's efforts to protect Norfolk.

Drizzle drowned the glow of twilight from the window where Simon stared at the steam rising from his cup of chocolate in Miller's Ordinary. The innkeeper's daughter placed a candle on the table next to his open book. The girl took the time to smile at him while she brought flame to wick. Simon nodded his thanks and looked down at the open page. He'd been on the same page for three days.

Images of his friend's wedding played across his mind. A jubilant Field couldn't keep his gaze off his new wife, Delany, resplendent in a silver gown. Field had been jubilant. And seeing Field always reminded Simon of Amity. Their features were similar, the same brown hair that glowed red in the sun, but Amity's eyes were the color of a storm on the bay. Would Amity be jubilant on her wedding day? Sharing secret smiles with her husband that she thought no one else would see? He hoped he'd never see it.

"Mind if I join ye?" A full tankard sloshed on to the table. Simon snatched his book from the running puddle. Above him stood a barrel-chested man. Blue eyes glowed from a weather-wrinkled face.

"Captain John McCabe." The man reached a dirty hand across the table.

A welcome diversion for thoughts sliding in the wrong direction, Simon shook the man's hand warmly. The next hour passed quickly as Simon listened to the story of Captain McCabe's latest voyage across the Atlantic.

"Our Tom was a sorry lad. Coming home after his education," the captain leaned in, "he told me how he'd found how to get anything he ever wanted, so he was coming home."

"Everything he ever wanted?" Simon hoped his smile didn't drip with the cynicism he felt, the memory of soft storm-colored eyes twinkled at him.

"Sure. That's what he told me and then he showed me this." The Captain pulled from his pocket a medallion of clear green stone. It spun like a coin and came to rest across from Simon. Could this be a gemstone? It was the largest he'd ever seen, spanning nearly three of his fingers. The room was too dim to make out the carving in the center. The candlelight reflected off its polished surface like dark window glass.

A little arc of excitement sparked to life in a remote memory of Simon's brain and shivered down his spine. "Is this what I think it is? May I?"

McCabe shrugged.

Simon reached for the stone. Cool and smooth to the touch, the hatch-like carvings were barely perceptible under his thumb though they did not appear worn.

"What do you think it is?"

"I'm not sure, but there are legends about ancient stones."

"This couldn't be one of them stones. My cousin Tom didn't travel in them kinda circles. It's nothing but a piece of junk he picked up somewhere," he laughed, "but Tom'd believe just about anything you told him. Some scoundrel told him a fanciful tale, and he believed it. Gave all his money, poor sod."

A cool disappointment breezed through Simon. "You're probably right. I mean what are the odds that a regular person would come across something like that when people have been looking for it for centuries?" Even as he said it, the possibility niggled. Excitement deepened.

The captain took a long swig from his cup. "And regular he was and no mistake. And all the money he had would have been a couple of pounds. Now I've got to take his things to his mother. It's a visit I would avoid if it were possible. You have family?"

"My mother and father passed away a few years ago."

"No wife?"

"I have a sister."

The captain grimaced. "Maybe I should give you this stone. Our Tom believed it would do him some good, maybe it *will* do for ye."

Simon reluctantly laid the stone back in the center of the table. "You should keep it or give it to his mother. Perhaps it will bring you all you ever wanted."

"I've got what I want, lad." A knowing smile wrinkled his face. "My wife is waiting for me at home with four boys. And what Tom's mother will want no rock can do."

Simon nodded his agreement. No stone would give him what he wanted either. Although if it were the right stone it could add significantly to his knowledge of electricity. There was nothing to be lost in giving it a try. "I'll buy your dinner in exchange for the stone."

McCabe smiled, "You, too?"

"I don't think it will get me everything I want, but I do think it would make an interesting scientific experiment."

"Whatever you say, me lad." McCabe stood on unsteady legs and tossed the stone to Simon. "I'll be on me way."

Simon nodded to the Captain. Smooth and cool to

the touch, the stone slipped into his pocket without a catch. He closed his book, turned toward the stairwell and his room. From his right, in a corner of the room a shout of "huzzah" and the clink of raised goblets grabbed his notice. Near the bar, a young man knocked sideways through the thinning crowd as he pushed his way out of the Ordinary. When Simon looked forward again, he found a pair of stormy eyes. "What are you doing here?" He put his hand in his pocket. Was the stone warm? No, it wasn't possible. Was it? No, it must be warming due to the heat of embarrassment.

"…tomorrow." She smiled at him though her gaze showed turbulence.

"I'm sorry." He stumbled. "I missed what you said."

Her smile changed to one of an indulgent nanny. "I said I am awaiting the arrival of my father tomorrow morning. We are going to Williamsburg for the Committee."

Suddenly his mind gained clear focus. He took note of the soldiers in the corner. He took her elbow and led her toward the stairs. "You mean you are here alone?"

"Of course not."

His tension eased a smidge.

"Lucy is here."

Tension resumed its upward climb.

"My father arrives in the morning. Honestly Simon, there is nothing to worry about. Why are you here?"

"Let me see you to your room."

Exasperation wearied her countenance. "It's hardly necessary. I can find my way myself. In fact, I was just on my way."

"Well that is convenient, because I am headed in the same direction." He smiled at her.

She grimaced.

He waved her up the stairs. "After you, Miss Archer."

She huffed up the stairs.

Simon couldn't stifle his grin.

"I'm grown woman, Simon Morgan."

Yes. He could see that in the sway of her hips as she took each step with precision. "Perhaps I will see you and your father in the morning. I hope you sleep well." He knew better than to grin in her face, but he couldn't help it. Hat in hand, he waited in the hallway until she closed her door. To her credit, she closed the door quietly. Hester would have slammed it, and where she was be hanged. Simon stepped into his own room.

Stuffed into the room with a canopied bed was a small ladder-backed chair and a little writing table. Leaving the door ajar, Simon placed his book on the table, adjusted the chair to face the doorway, and lit the candle. After retrieving his ink and turning to a fresh page in his notebook, he proceeded to write down everything he could remember about how he came to be in possession of what could be the Horeb Stone.

Simon looked up when Amity's light went out under the crack at the bottom of her door. His own candle sputtered. He retrieved another candle from his pouch. For the first time in days, he was able to concentrate on work he'd placed before himself. Amity had haunted his thoughts since her brother's wedding. Knowing she was safe in the next room dreaming, as long as he didn't think about what those dreams might be, freed him to wonder about the artifact placed before him on the table.

Held up to the candle the odd reflectiveness receded. Clear green water. The kind of water one could breathe under in a dream. Light reflected off the lines of the center carving. Obviously, an ancient language of lines and crossed lines, Hebrew? He ran his thumb over the center carving. More indented than carved and no wear appeared on the edges.

Halfway into his second candle and his list of everything he could remember of the properties of the stone, a horse arrived in the yard. Simon placed his rifle on his lap and resumed writing. Whispers downstairs floated incomplete to his ear. Simon placed the quill in the ink pot. Boots scraped on the stairs. Simon positioned the rifle on the table toward the opening in the door.

Reed Archer, Amity's father, came into view.

Simon moved the rifle to his lap.

Reed pointed to the door behind him.

Simon nodded.

Reed nodded back.

Simon closed his door and went to bed.

3

Simon stood up at his table to greet Amity and her father when they walked into the chamber for breakfast.

"Reed, you're down early this morning. I thought you wouldn't be down for some hours yet," Simon said.

Amity stifled a roll of her eyes. She'd hoped he'd be gone by now.

"Good to see you, Simon." The men shook hands. "No, I've got to get to the committee in Williamsburg today."

"Please, have a seat." Simon gestured to the table moving aside the gazette he'd been reading.

After placing their request for coffee and the diet, Amity's Papa sat back in his chair, thumbs crooked in the pockets of his waistcoat. "I have received a note from the Glassock's. They have removed from Williamsburg for the duration. It seems Mrs. Glassock is from Norfolk, and the burning scared her witless. Not that she was abundant in wits to begin with, but she is a kind woman, and Hugh could have done much worse. At any rate, they are not here, and so we are absent a companion for Amity while I am here."

Simon turned to address her. "You must be

disappointed."

"Yes. Well, as I have only just heard it myself, I have not had sufficient time to work up any emotion at all. And I have Auntie Clementine."

"Yes, but she is hardly good company for a young girl." Papa interjected.

"I'm hardly a girl, Papa."

"Well, you are not a man." He chuckled and sought to draw Simon into his joke.

Simon smiled, but his gaze darted to Amity. Was he trying to gauge her reaction? That was new. In times past, she couldn't get his attention without placing herself in mortal danger.

"Amity has romantic notions about the mountains."

Amity took a deep breath, let it out, and then smiled at the two men. It was no use arguing that one. It never went past an announcement that she was soft-headed like all those of her sex. She hated to think what he would have been like if her formidable mother had not shattered his illusions of the frailty of the female mind and creativity.

Too bad that Robertine Glassock couldn't attend her on this trip. Robbie knew all the good places to go to hear about traveling to the mountains. She'd ascertained a route from here, but how to get there? There were so many things to think and plan and no Robbie to help her.

"Do you wish to go west, Amity?" Simon looked intrigued as though he'd recently discovered she had a brain between her ears.

"She's heard enough discouraging tales of Indians and what they do to settlers up there." Papa turned his pointed gaze to her. "It's no place for a girl."

"Have you read of the missions up there?" Amity countered. "Women labor beside their husbands. It's important work."

"Husband. That's the key." He pounded his finger on the table. "Once you marry you can travel the world. Right now, I have to protect you."

"Not everyone is meant to marry, Papa. There are single ladies at the mission. They live together in a separate house. You will have Simon thinking that women are good for nothing but decoration."

"I sincerely doubt that anyone married to your mother would think anything of the kind."

"Or my sister." Simon grinned, and a mischievous twinkle lit his eyes. "I promise you; I think much more of women than that."

Amity was glad to hear it. Perhaps, some day he would make someone a good husband. A woman who could capture his attention, at least one that wouldn't mind if he forgot about her now and then.

"What brings you to Williamsburg, Morgan?"

"A letter from John Parchment." Earnestness replaced the twinkle. "The Virginian Society of the Promotion of Usefull Knowledge is hosting a demonstration of electricity at Charleton's coffee shop."

"Surely they cannot plan to continue meeting in the middle of a war?"

"I hear they are suspended, but Ritter is coming to

demonstrate his electrical battery."

"Fascinating stuff, but hardly useful."

Simon's countenance switched. It was a look unique to him. Almost wistful, but the cogs of his mind turned double-time when he got that look, so much that he forgot much that surrounded him. "It's true." Simon's hands began to punctuate his speech, "But what if we could harness the light? Perhaps we could use it for surgeries and other things."

Amity's heart tugged a memory from the long ago, moonless night of Simon's parents' carriage accident. His father, Jacob Morgan, died instantly. His injured wife survived the journey home only to die while a surgeon worked on her wounds. The doctor lamented throughout the entire procedure of the lack light.

Papa fell silent.

"Perhaps it will after all, my boy."

Amity smiled. Her Papa wasn't all bluster. At least, not all of the time. The pause allowed them a chance to taste their breakfast.

"Since you are here, would you mind if I asked you to help me keep an eye on Amity? Her friends are not here, and I would be grateful for an old family friend such as yourself to attend her when I cannot."

Amity choked on her coffee. "I don't require a chaperone when I attend parties at home, why only last week Patience and I travelled to Pine's Wold for a party."

"You aren't at home."

"Papa." She lowered her voice almost a whisper, "We wouldn't wish to give people the wrong impression."

"What?" her father chuckled. "If your brother were here, I would ask him—since he is not and Simon is very like a brother to you, what could be the harm?"

"Papa."

"If Simon were interested in you, he would have offered years ago. Nothing to worry about."

Amity was sure she would combust from the heat racing all over her body to collect in her face. What could cause Papa to say such a thing in public? He'd always been plainspoken, but—

Simon, stiff as one of Mama's carvings, moved only his eyes back and forth between them, finally settling on her father. "I would be delighted to escort Amity, sir."

That was worse. Surely her father could understand humiliation. How could the two of them ever have a normal conversation again?

"Please forgive me Simon, but surely it won't be necessary. My father is here, and I shall have Auntie Clementine."

"With the number of soldiers about it might be best if I send you home directly. I don't know what your mother was about agreeing to your coming with me at such a time."

"No." She grabbed control of her voice before she shouted. "I mean, we will be at Aunt Clementine's, so I won't be out and about too often. I shall be safe. And since Simon has agreed to act as my brother, we should fare well."

"I daresay I will be busy. I had a note from Patrick.

There is much to be done. General Lee is on his way."

Peace eased in over her qualms, perhaps this would work in her favor. No doubt, her parents hoped she'd find a husband in Williamsburg. She smiled into her cup. The likelihood that she would find someone suitable would be significantly reduced with Simon hovering around. Simon Morgan, though scholarly, looked anything but. He was tall like her brother, slighter build, but equally strong. Amity had seen them spar, and Simon came out on top at least as often as Field did. It shouldn't be too hard to think of Simon as her brother. The feelings she had for him had been a girlhood fantasy. She was immune to his charm now. He was her brother's best friend. He had always been around, just like a brother. *Only he wasn't.*

4

Simon rolled the stone in his hand as he steered his mount toward Williamsburg. He'd been so stunned by Reed's request he didn't dare move lest any movement would break the charm. Reed was obviously unaware of Amity's declaration five years ago that they would not suit. Mortification painted Amity's lovely cheeks like firelight. Well, one had to crack a nut to get to the meat inside. The shell she'd placed around herself had been breached by no less than her father. Outrageously done, but done, nonetheless.

Could it be the influence of the stone? He'd seen Amity more in the past twenty-four hours than he had in the past year. If he ever saw McCabe again, Simon would be sure to thank him. Rotten luck his nephew had died—he might have been onto something, after all. As soon as he dropped his things at Anderson's Tavern, he would head to the library at William and Mary to investigate further what was known of the stone.

Once in Williamsburg, he dodged traffic on Duke of Gloucester Street through wood-fire scented wind. A cloud of warm air enveloped him upon entry to the tavern. In the large chamber to his right several tables of soldiers partook of the day's tavern fare. In the far doorway, Mr. Anderson stood by his desk. Simon was spared crossing the room when Anderson hailed and threaded his way through the tables toward the entrance.

"Welcome back, Mr. Morgan." Anderson raised his voice to be heard over the din of shirtmen.

Simon glanced over the innkeeper's shoulder at boisterous outbursts.

"Harmless talk. Don't mind them. They've come for their dinner."

"What is for dinner today?"

"Our diet for today is as posted: ham stew and bread. There's apple syllabub if you've a care for it. Of course, for you, Mr. Morgan, we can accommodate a larger selection."

Simon's stomach answered for him. "Stew sounds good. I will take it in the parlor."

Anderson nodded and shouted for a young boy to carry Simon's case to his room.

Simon followed. Once settled in his room he retrieved his copy of *Common Sense* and headed back downstairs to eat before he walked to John Parchment's house. Instead, he found John reclining with a cup of coffee in Anderson's exclusive parlor.

"Morgan!" Parchment stood and offered his hand. "I heard Anderson shout, but I didn't know it was the right Morgan."

"Parchment." Simon took the offered hand, "I was coming to see you. What brings you out?"

"A house full of women in a fuss since midmorning. A friend of my wife's is visiting from Fredericksburg."

Envy tinged Simon's good will for his old friend. He had his sister, but a large family full of laughter met his ideal of the future, and for the first time in a very long time, it seemed it might be possible.

"You don't know because you don't have any children yet. Four daughters," he laid his hand over his heart, eyes heavenward. "They are my blessings." He dropped his gaze toward Simon. "And the bane of my existence." He took a deep swig of his draught. "This friend of my wife's has come to attend the Society meeting."

"Will they allow a woman in Charlton's?"

"I had to call in a favor or two. Old Walden hasn't given me an answer yet, but I don't think he'll be a problem because he will not be in attendance himself."

"Must be some friend."

John nodded. "Sarah and Winifred grew up next to each other in Fredericksburg. Winifred is interested in the healing powers of electricity."

A young lad of fourteen or so stepped quietly into the room with a large tray and placed a full bowl of stew, a small, crusty loaf of bread, a plate of syllabub, and a steaming dish of coffee. "There ye are, sir."

"Thank you."

Simon asked a silent blessing for his food and waited for the boy to retreat before he spoke again. "John, I want to meet with someone from the NTSS."

Parchment looked to the door of the parlor. Simon followed his look.

"Why do you wish to speak to the 'Never Tells'? What makes you think I can help you?"

Simon startled at his response. John never sought praise, only commiseration for his four daughters. "If anyone knows it's you. You're still connected to the college and you live here. Who else would I ask?"

"If such a clandestine group existed—and I'm not saying it does…"

Simon swallowed a piece of bread dipped in the spicy stew. "The devil, John. I'm not interested in secret society nonsense."

"They are serious things, Simon. The people in them take them very seriously, indeed."

Simon raised his eyebrows. "I have a matter to discuss with someone of more knowledge than myself of certain objects. How am I to find out anything if they hide themselves from public view?"

Parchment closed the door and resumed his seat. "What type of object?"

"It's a stone." Simon pulled the amulet from his pocket and placed it on the table.

Parchment squinted at it while rubbing his hands on his thighs. "The Horeb Stone?"

"I'm not sure, but it might be." Simon tingled with excitement. In the twenty-four hours since he'd taken possession of the stone, he'd no one to share the possibilities with.

"Have you seen any unusual events in connection with the stone?"

Simon held back his suspicions. They were only what he'd surmised, and twenty-four hours was hardly enough time to analyze anything. "Nothing solid."

"Have you seen it glow?"

"I have not observed it myself, but I have kept it in my pocket since I acquired it yesterday."

"One legend says that if you ask it a question it will glow for an affirmative answer."

Simon reeled. Was that why it had been warm in his pocket? Had it been sensing his questions and affirming his suspicions?

Parchment sat back and laced his fingers over his middle. "You need to keep it quiet. People don't cotton to the occult."

"It's hardly devil worship."

"What else would you call it? Enchanted stones. Magic. Fires?"

"When you put it that way, I see your point. That is why I need to speak to an expert."

"My only suggestion is that you do not miss the Society's meeting on Friday evening at Charlton's."

Simon returned to a congealed, tepid stew when Parchment left him for home. He'd never considered that his friend might be a member of the group he sought. He certainly knew more about the stone than he let on.

5

Gusts of wind rocked the carriage on its springs, but no matter. The sun was shining, and Amity was on her way to Williamsburg at last. Dancing, shopping, parties, and whatever else Aunt Clementine planned for her visit. During the night ideas formed for a little pamphlet, she thought to produce of her visit. Her father was right. War was upon them; surely, people would like to know the happenings of the capital during a war. Unfortunately, she had little time to write when she visited her aunt. This time she would simply have to make time to keep careful notes.

Amity sat next to her father in their chariot. A bundled Lucy perched next to the driver. Once out of the coach yard, Amity took a deep breath and placed a smile on her face. "Papa—"

"I know what you are going to say. I meant what I said, Amity. Simon Morgan will escort you, or I will send you home directly, and you will stay there for the duration."

Irritation spiked. "How do you suppose you will accomplish that? Surely, Aunt has plans. It's not as if we lived next to each other as we do at home."

"Morgan will stay at Anderson's. I will send for him and give him a list of your engagements as soon as you have completed it."

"But—"

"No more." He sighed and patted her knee. "It has been a long night." He turned toward the window.

Aunt Clementine, who was actually her father's aunt and her great-aunt, would admit to being six-foot tall, but everyone knew she was at least a couple of inches taller than that with a personality to match.

"Papa, no one would dare cross Aunt Clementine."

"We are at war. Even Clementine, as formidable as she may seem, is no match for a man half her size." Papa yawned.

What she would give for her pen. Nowhere else could she explode safely.

Within minutes, Papa's breathing evened. He would sleep all the way to Williamsburg.

Amity's heart warmed as she listened to the rhythm. He was her own father, dear soul. He only wanted what was best for her, but she couldn't help her agitation. When would he realize she needed to make her own decisions? She turned her gaze toward the plantations and the river rolling past her window.

The coach neared the outskirts of a town and then rolled down a street. A row of white houses with black shutters next to the road announced their arrival in Williamsburg.

Amity eagerly scanned the landscape as energy from the city hummed around and through her.

On Francis Street, the driver stopped to allow a group of ladies to cross the street.

Papa woke. "What. Here already?"

Amity nodded, her smile wide.

He patted her knee. "You always did love the city, my girl. You get that from your mama."

Her excitement created a euphoria in her heart that threatened forgiveness for everyone and everything that had ever gone wrong in her entire life. Her cheeks ached from smiling as they pulled up in front of Aunt Clementine's.

After knocking and waiting several minutes, they let themselves in.

Servants bustled from room to room.

Aunt Clementine, dressed in her own hair, rather than a white wig, and an indigo mantua with a pale green petticoat, sat on her throne directing the madness. "Good afternoon, Reed. You came just in time. I've decided I'm leaving." She reached for him to place a kiss in the air near his cheek.

"Clementine." Amity's father greeted her. "Did you just tell me that you are leaving?"

The lace in her cap fluttered with the violence of her affirmative gesture. "Yes. Reed, you did hear me correctly."

"But where will you be going?"

"I intend to sail for Europe."

"Have you gained permission from the Continental Congress for such a trip?"

"Don't be silly. What do they have to do with anything?"

Papa turned from her aunt, hat, and gloves still in hand, and laid them on an empty chair. Once he'd shifted out of his great coat, he turned back to her and spoke again. "You need to request permission to sail to Europe. If you do, they will likely think you are a Tory. If you are a Tory, they will detain you. If they let you leave, you likely will not be able to return. You're not a Tory, are you, Clementine?"

She huffed. "Of course not!" She plopped back down on one of two large, throne-like chairs behind her. If Aunt Clementine was six-feet tall, Uncle William was six-and-a-half feet. He'd commissioned the chairs for the two of them after searching far and wide for anything comfortable for the two to sit on.

As if just noting her presence her aunt gazed her way. "Amity, my dear child, how fares your mother?"

"Well, Aunt. She wished to come to you but decided she was needed at home."

"I daresay you've been looking forward to this trip to town?"

"Yes, Aunt."

"Well, I shan't disappoint you as your father has disappointed me. Since I shan't be leaving with the next tide, I think we had better put our heads together and decide what we will do whilst you are here."

Amity threw her arms around her aunt. "Thank you, Aunt Clementine."

"You are most welcome, dear girl. Now up to your rooms. It's nearly time for dinner and I know you will want to freshen yourselves."

Amity shed her brown woolen traveling clothes for her lavender muslin gown. She took care to place paper and ink on the desk by the window. She must capture her thoughts today, perhaps if her things were out, she would be more apt to make the time necessary.

Dinner at Clementine's was always good. Today was no exception. Fricasseed chicken, turnips, bread, cheese, canned peaches.

"I'm afraid local travel is all you may have available to you at present, Clementine." Papa took another sip of soup. "I am willing to take you home with me when I leave at the end of the session. In the meantime, the two of you should make the most of town while you are here. I have arranged for an old family friend to escort you both when I cannot attend you."

Clementine bristled so hard that Amity thought her curls would straighten. "Reed Archer, do you presume to tell me what I may or may not do?"

Papa relaxed into his chair as his tone became even and soft. "Of course not, Clementine. But you cannot secure passage right now. And it's hard to say who our allies will be in this endeavor."

"Mr. Franklin is in Europe."

"Franklin is in Philadelphia. Besides which, Franklin is a powerful *man*."

"I will go to Barbados."

"Clementine. Really. If you must go, go to your sons. Or come to Archer Hall. Ann would love to see you. Go somewhere where you have family to protect you."

"I do not wish protection from adventure, Reed. Only armies."

"I hear Anderson is still hosting balls every week."

"You have heard correctly." Clementine shook her head. "I can't get the sight of Nero fiddling while Rome burned out of my head. What were the dear folks in Norfolk doing while this conflict raged around them? I expect the balls at Maury's continued as well."

Papa deflated. "Do what you will, Clementine, you will anyway."

"Precisely." Clementine softened in her victory. "Although you have given me a reason for a pause. What do you mean I cannot book passage?"

"The harbors are shut down. Surely you've heard the British navy has our ports blocked."

"All of them?"

"The important ones. Congress would have to give you leave, but they aren't likely to do that right now."

"Who is this person you have engaged to escort me through my own town?"

"His name is Simon Morgan. His plantation is next to my own."

"Are we encouraging him in his pursuit of our girl here?"

"No. If he wanted Amity, he'd have asked for her years ago."

Amity flamed. *Restraint is a virtue.* She fisted her napkin into a ball in her lap instead of throwing it into her plate. "Papa must you keep saying that?"

"Which is precisely why I asked him. He should stay out of the way should anyone else come along."

Amity shuddered and hoped the opposite was true. If she stuck to Simon perhaps, 'anyone else' would leave her alone. "Have you decided to stay then?"

"I've decided to think on it some more." Clementine conceded.

Papa looked relieved as he picked up his glass. "Wise, Clementine."

"Perhaps?" Amity shook with the thought.

Clementine turned toward her. "Yes, my dear?"

"What of the west? Perhaps the mountains?"

Papa stood up. "Amity. Your aunt is too old to be traipsing off to the mountains."

Clementine stood to face him; a full head taller than Papa with eyes as bright as Simon's electrical experiments.

"Excellent idea, my dear. It's about time I paid a visit to my very old friends, Jedediah and Evelyn Eberly in Winchester. Perhaps you would wish to accompany me?"

Papa's eyes widened.

Amity's heart thudded in her chest.

"Perhaps I will engage that young man, Mr. Morgan, to accompany us. What say you to that?"

"Are they the couple that you courted with?" Amity asked.

"Yes, Jedediah and Evelyn courted at the same time as William and I. William and Jedediah grew up together, they were like brothers. Jedediah wrote such a heartfelt letter when William passed, I knew it was time I went to see them."

"There is no use in telling you that such a trip could be dangerous."

"Nonsense, Reed. Traveling is always dangerous."

"Then, I will see you tomorrow. You--" he pointed at Amity "--I will see you in your Uncle William's library before you retire for the evening."

She nodded.

Papa walked deliberately away from the table.

Amity huffed a deep breath.

Clementine turned a sharp gaze toward her at the unladylike behavior.

"I don't mean that my parents aren't everything they are supposed to be. They are generous, kind— "

"And?"

"And they want me to marry before I am ready. I know I shall have to marry. And I truly wish to, but not before I've seen something of the world. What's wrong with that? There is no one suitable at home anyway. You must know what I mean. You have the freedom to do as you wish."

"How like your father you are." Clementine placed a cool hand over Amity's. "When your father said he would see you in William's library for an instant it felt as though my William might be in there still waiting for me." She patted Amity's hand and retreated. "Marriage is not a prison, my dear. There is rest in a good marriage, and freedom as well."

"If you say so, Aunt." She didn't believe it.

"And so we are clear, I will not be manipulated by your father, or you. Don't put me in the middle of the two of you again. I shan't defend you the next time."

"Yes, Aunt."

"Good. Let's have dessert and decide when we

want to leave for the mountains."

Amity enjoyed the brown betty dessert. But her father had waited long enough. She said good night to her aunt and approached Uncle William's library carrying a small plate of the confection. It was his favorite.

A brace of candles illuminated the gray of her father's temples. His quill scratched across a sheet of paper. "Sit down." He said without looking up from his letter.

Amity crossed the room and quietly placed the dessert on the desk before him. The fork tinkled when he pushed it away. Two stuffed leather chairs stood before the desk. She balanced on the edge of one as he fixed her with his gaze.

"What are you about? Can you not see what dangerous times we are living in?"

"Aunt Clementine says I remind her of you."

"You remind me of your mother, and that is what scares me." He came out from around the desk and sat on a settee placed under a window. The glass reflected a wavy version of herself. She took a seat next to him to avoid the distraction of watching herself.

"Annie always had a mind of her own and the determination to make her own way in the world."

"What do you mean? Surely I've done nothing wrong."

"Amity, the things that you are searching for are at home."

"How will I ever know that? How can I be content to stay in one place all my life if I've never experienced its opposite? Did you know the Eberlys left twenty years ago to build themselves a home in the wilderness?" Her arms prickled in gooseflesh.

Her father nodded his head up and down rolling his eyes. "And my telling you isn't enough."

"No."

"We have raised you with too much freedom."

"I think not."

"You would do. Happiness does not come from outside yourself. It comes from inside as you learn to be thankful for what you have."

"I am thankful for everything you have ever done for me. I feel as though I will bust if I don't get out of here. I wish to see the mountains. At least once before I'm staked down by the skirt with the needs of children."

"What will I tell your mother? That I let you go traipsing off into Indian territory alone with your crazy aunt?"

"Winchester is hardly Indian territory. It's a town now. Aunt Clementine said she will ask Simon to attend us. Do you think he will?"

"It depends on how long you expect to be gone. The ground is still too cold for planting. He may be able to manage it, but not for long."

Amity sat quietly waiting for her father to say yes. She'd felt it coming the way she'd always been able to tell that he was giving in.

"Are you prepared for all the consequences that may result from such an adventure?"

"Yes. I mean, I'm fairly certain. I know that my

book may fail, but without taking a risk I will never know."

He looked as if she'd slapped him. "This is about a book you want to write?"

"Of course." She swung her palm out in front of herself. "*A Diary of the Western Mountains* by Amity Archer. Of course I'm open to better titles."

"You miss my point. Yes, your book might fail, although I doubt it. Your mother and I have always known you had a way of the phrase about you."

She warmed at his praise and leaned in to rest her head on his shoulder. "Thank you, Papa. Right now, I am working on my thoughts of Williamsburg at war. Do you think you could take me to see the troops?"

He held her briefly then turned to face her. "The troops? One thing at a time. Do you realize that you may be compromised and forced to marry on this trip?"

She snorted. "I very seriously doubt it. After all, Simon will be there. You know he will take care of me, just like Field. He always has. Just like Field."

"Do you dislike him so much?"

She hesitated a fraction of a heartbeat before telling the truth. Perhaps the truth would help him understand that she was capable of making her own decisions. "No. I loved him once, but I know we will never suit."

Her father stared. "It's just as well that he didn't offer for you then."

"Yes. I would hate to hurt him, but how could I be married to someone who forgets my existence?"

"No one could ever forget your existence, my dear child." He took her hand. "I must have the answer to this question: do you understand that you may very well have to marry Simon Morgan if things go wrong on this journey?"

Surely not. Aunt Clementine and Lucy would be there. All would be well. "Yes. I understand that if things go horribly wrong, I will have to marry him." Amity shuddered. Nothing that exciting *ever* happened. She would be vigilant and Aunt Clementine doubly so— she always was.

"And you accept that risk. There will be no turning back."

Amity let out a deep breath. "Yes."

6

Simon swallowed the last of his bread and cheese as Reed walked into the parlor at Anderson's.

Reed placed a portfolio on the table. "I've brought a list of engagements that Amity and her aunt are planning to attend. I have marked on them the ones I will attend myself, which you can see is most of them." Reed slid the list across the table.

Simon glanced over the busy schedule.

"I shall require your assistance on three or four evenings if you are still amenable." Reed took a seat and declined a cup of coffee. Tomorrow night Amity would need Simon to attend a party at the Peytons'. A singular thing to see you guarding my daughter's door. You *were* guarding her door, were you not?"

Simon nodded, "Yes, sir. The crowd below consisted of rowdy shirtmen worse for drink. I thought it best."

"Yes, well, my delay could not be helped. My foreman wanted correcting before he destroyed my sheep."

Simon remained silent. It wouldn't help his suit one bit to tell her father just what he thought about sending his daughter alone to stay in a common ordinary for all that he had regained her closer acquaintance. "Yes. I understand your sentiment." Simon didn't move.

"I thought it was like that."

"Sir?" Talking to Reed was often like that; he was always a thought or two ahead of where Simon thought he was.

"You'll speak to me when you're ready, eh? Well." Reed rose and collected his portfolio. "I can respect that. Until then I must be off."

Simon had planned to call on Amity tomorrow morning, but it would have to be today. The meeting of the Society was paramount. Before it was a matter of curiosity, now it was regarding the stone. He would need to find out the particulars of the party to determine how he could do both.

As he crossed the commons and made his way to Amity's aunt's home, a brisk wind blew the warmth of the sun toward the river.

Simon was escorted into a large parlor lined with burgundy paper. At one end, a very tall woman rose from a most extraordinary chair.

Amity joined him from somewhere off to the side. "Aunt Clementine, may I introduce Mr. Simon Morgan."

"You noticed my throne." A twinkle sparked her hazel eyes, which were level with his own.

"Ma'am."

"My husband had it made for me. We are tall. And none of those flimsy things will quite suffice for real sitting."

Simon had to smile. Was there such a thing as

pretend sitting? Though in fairness he did know what she meant about the fragility and shortness of chairs.

"My William was a kind man, Mr. Morgan."

He must have been.

Amity offered him a seat across from her on a chair. She perched on a settee.

Outside a carriage wheeled by.

"Reed tells me that you have offered to escort us on our outings?"

"That is precisely why I came to call. I came to inquire about the time and place of your party this evening. I have an important prior engagement and wish to ascertain if I may attend both."

"Have no fear on our account, Mr. Morgan. Mr. Peyton, whose mother is hosting this evening's soiree, will be present. He has shown particular interest in my niece, and I am sure he will be most happy to oblige our safety."

Amity's cheeks glowed anew with blush. Was it because of the proposed intentions of Peyton?

"I'll be there." He heard himself say before he'd thought.

Amity's gaze darted to his, this time lit with a teasing sparkle. "I understand it's a card party, Simon."

"Shall we play backgammon?" He'd noted that the indigo of her gown matched the subtle stormy blue of her eyes.

She answered with a broad smile. "If you think you could stand losing to me again."

"We'll see about that."

"We shall be ready at five, Mr. Morgan."

Simon took the hint, rose from his chair, and bowed to both ladies. "It will be my pleasure to see you then, ma'am."

Amity walked him to the door. "My father appreciates the time you are taking to escort us, Simon."

"He is very welcome, as are you." Her eyes were serious now, all teasing faded.

"That is what I wish to discuss with you."

His interest peaked, could this be the work of the stone? A chance to speak with Amity hadn't happened in a very long time.

"I don't wish to marry yet, Simon."

Or not.

"Don't you?"

"No. And, since we know that we will not suit, you are the perfect person to help me."

Bewildered he could only ask, "What?"

"Papa has asked you to escort me to keep me safe. I am asking you to help me keep all suitors away. Just as my brother would."

"I don't think Field tries to keep *all* suitors away from you Amity. Just the unsuitable ones." He almost grinned at his pun, but the seriousness of her countenance checked his tone.

"Maybe not. But I want you to."

"All of them?"

"Yes."

"You are absolutely sure about this?"

"Yes."

"I shall do what I can."

Her face opened into a smile that set all his circuits humming.

"I am sorry you will miss your meeting tonight."

Simon was not sorry at all. He'd been so focused on the stone and its possible power that it wasn't until Clementine had mentioned Will Peyton that Simon realized that other men would likely pursue Amity. And now he had her permission to drive them off? "I wouldn't miss this game of backgammon for the world."

~*~

"Will you ask him tonight?" Amity asked.

"Not yet. I want to see what manner of man he is before I decide to travel with him that far and for that long."

"Papa says Simon will not be able to be gone for very long due to the start of the planting season."

"Of course not. We still have time. I calculate that it will take us no longer than a week to get to Winchester. I do not suppose we could imposition them for longer than a week or two, then we will have to travel back home. All in all, I think a month, maybe six weeks, should do it. I wrote to Evelyn this morning to let them know we will be coming."

Amity breathed deep. Simon should be able to manage that, surely.

Winchester perched on the very edge of the wilderness. Yet they could make it there by taking the

King's Highway. She and Clementine would ride in the coach the whole way. It wouldn't be comfortable, but it would be an adventure. She had so much to plan for, first on her list was a trip to the printing office. She must have a new notebook, perhaps two, for this journey.

7

A thrill vibrated through Amity at the sight of Simon filling the doorway. His chestnut hair was smoothed into a black curlew. The deep forest green of his coat matched flecks of green in his hazel eyes.

"Mrs. Foster. Miss Archer. Shall we?" Simon bowed, and then winged an arm to her aunt.

Aunt Clementine nodded her agreement before taking his arm with a smile.

Amity followed down the steps to the waiting carriage. A crisp wind tickled her nose.

After handing Aunt into the carriage, Simon turned to Amity. Strength and confidence radiated through the steadiness of his hand. An echo of a long-ago dance caught her fancy.

"Nice night for party." Simon offered when they were seated and rolling down the street.

"Yes, Mr. Morgan." Aunt agreed before Amity could speak. Clementine carried the conversation.

Amity gazed out the window at the bustling city. A periwinkle twilight edged the corners of the houses they passed. Long ago, she'd dreamt of taking Simon's hand and walking in the evening while golden light shone out of the windows. To talk of family things in hushed tones. An old girlish fancy no doubt recalled by the echo of that dance. But that was old news.

A short ride later, they pull up in front of the Peytons' home.

Simon alighted first and offered his assistance to her aunt. He then held his hand out to Amity, but just as their fingertips touched, someone spoke. Simon swung around

"Morgan, I thought you to be at the Society meeting this evening. Traveled here for that purpose, did you not?" A man gave Simon a perplexed once over.

Simon stepped across the front of the carriage door blocking her exit. Forgotten so soon. So much for that. What did it matter? Her future didn't have space for such old dreams. She needed to concentrate on her readers. What would they like to hear about Williamsburg? Writing was a much safer place for her heart.

"Fletcher." The two men shook hands. "I was supposed to attend, but other matters kept me from it. I hope to meet with Dr. Ritter another time."

"I see you have much finer company with you than mine," Fletcher said, gesturing to the carriage. "I'll see you inside then."

Simon turned once more toward her and offered his hand. "Shall we?"

She took Simon's hand and gingerly stepped down. Her body betrayed her by pumping up its heartbeats and sending little gnats to stir up her insides. "Thank you, Simon." She said with as little emotion as possible so not to give him, or her rebellious heart, the wrong impression. With all her aunt's talk of Will Peyton and Simon, she would need to be on her guard not to show favor to either of them, or she'd find herself following a minister before she could say George Washington.

"My dear Clementine." Mrs. Peyton stood next to her husband in the great hall to greet their guests. Candlelight gleamed off the black and white checked floor. Guests mingled, mixing into the parlor and back to the hall again.

"How do you fare, Grace?" Not waiting for an answer Clementine went on. "I'd like to introduce Simon Morgan."

Behind them, the turquoise papered parlor glowed in candlelight. Small tables of slightly differing shapes, but adequate to seat four were sprinkled about the room.

Will Peyton, dressed in blue jersey wool with polished brass buttons stood when she entered. "Miss Archer—" he flourished a bow "—it is a pleasure to see you again."

"Mr. Peyton, I do not believe you are acquainted with our old friend, Simon Morgan."

"Mr. Morgan."

"Peyton." The men nodded to each other.

"Mr. Peyton, you look very military this evening."

"I've raised a regiment. We shall be leaving shortly to support our noble general. What about you, Morgan? Leading your militia, I daresay."

"Not as yet. Carter has the militia in hand and has not had a need for me."

"Mr. Morgan's plantations will call him home soon. Surely some of our men must stay home, how else will we feed our army, Mr. Peyton?"

Simon stiffened. A red flush crept up his neck.

"Indeed." Peyton nodded.

"I will fight when the time comes."

Peyton nodded again.

Amity's mind raced. Would he? A vision of Simon in danger clenched her stomach. How had she not seen this? She, who prided herself on seeing all sides of an argument. Of course he would fight. Clasping her hands in front of her waist kept them from landing on his arm when she looked at him.

Will swept his arm in a large arc toward the gaming tables. "Would you honor me with a game of backgammon?"

The question brought her back to the room. "Of course, Mr. Peyton."

~*~

Simon nodded stiffly once again and stepped away as Amity followed Mr. Peyton to an empty table for two.

"Mr. Morgan, would you care for a game of whist?"

He turned to see Clementine's wizened hazel eyes. He would prefer to abscond off to the Society meeting, but he couldn't refuse Aunt Clementine.

"Certainly."

He took his seat, which afforded him a view of

Amity over her aunt's shoulder.

"I believe Mr. Parchment expected you at the Society meeting, Mr. Morgan." The voice on his right came from Sarah Parchment.

"Yes. I had planned it so myself, but my old friends are in town, and so here I am."

"My nephew is concerned about us traveling out with so many soldiers about." Clementine piped in.

"It does him credit, I daresay, to make sure you are cared for, Clementine."

Clementine shuffled the deck and began to deal the cards. "Indeed. And so vexing."

Sarah's partner, sitting to his left puckered a sardonic smile. Whom did she mock? Certainly not him, he'd only just sat down.

"I apologize, Mr. Morgan. This is my good friend, Mrs. Blackstone."

"Oh, I understand you hail from Fredericksburg?"

Once again, a puckered smile distorted her looks. "I arrived a couple of days ago."

Simon glanced over Clementine's shoulder to see candlelight glisten in the curls bouncing around Amity's laughing face. He was too far to see the exact color of her eyes as they changed with the conversation.

"I understand you are interested in electricity, Mr. Morgan."

He swiveled back to the lady on his left.

"Yes. I am."

"I have recently completed Mr. Franklin's treatise on the subject myself."

"Really Winifred? Whatever for?" Sarah exclaimed over his own surprise.

"It's quite fascinating, Sarah."

Simon looked closer at Mrs. Blackstone. Skin of porcelain, eyes like iron. She was easy to look at, but he wondered if she'd ever known real joy. The mordant look of her smile said she hadn't.

"Not to me. I let John be interested in those things. I'm much too busy dealing with house and home."

"Sarah," her friend chided, "you sound like nothing outside of diapers catches your interest when I know for a fact you speak several languages."

"What say you," Clementine interrupted, "Mr. Morgan? Do you like education in a female?"

"I fail to see what gender has to do with it, ma'am. Anyone with an intellectual interest in a subject should be free to pursue it. Within reason, of course."

"Of course." Clementine nodded what he thought was her approval.

"I myself must make time for planting and harvesting. Then, of course, there are other familial duties that prevent the pleasure of indulging in intellectual pursuits."

"We must eat."

"Yes, and we must raise our children and provide for our families."

He let his gaze stray to Amity for a mere second. A gleam in the eye of Amity's aunt told him it wasn't lost on Clementine.

"Surely the pursuit of natural science—like electricity—makes the lives of our families better."

Mrs. Blackstone punctuated with a spade to the top of the growing pile in the center of the table with a snap and a pointed smirk.

"It is a vocation to add to knowledge for our understanding's sake," Simon said.

"Particularly in the medical field. There is such suffering in families from the lack of knowledge."

"I've often thought that something as simple as better light could have an enormous impact."

"It is the simple things, I find, that have unpredictable results—profound results." Mrs. Blackstone kept her gaze on the cards before her.

Simon agreed. "You must be the friend that John invited to the Association meeting tonight."

Mrs. Blackstone stopped.

"Indeed I was." She resumed snapping a card on the top of the pile. "But my dear friend Sarah was coming to this party, and John got resistance at every turn. I decided I should rather spend the evening with people who welcomed my company."

Simon could only agree.

"Have you conducted any electrical experiments on artifacts?"

"Artifacts, Mrs. Blackstone?"

"Yes. I've heard that certain old items when treated with electricity produce almost magical results." She skewered him with her iron eyes.

She couldn't know about the stone, could she?

"Do you have any particular artifact in mind?"

She demurred, glancing down at the cards in her hand. "I've heard legends and rumors that such things exist."

He shrugged his shoulders. "I've often found that such legends have no basis in scientific fact."

"There are many things that are true that appear to have no basis in scientific fact."

He shrugged again and looked at his two remaining cards. "Perhaps we haven't understood, yet."

"Perhaps." She conceded and that odd puckered smile distorted her face once again.

~*~

It wouldn't work. Simon could not keep possible suitors away if he played cards all evening with strange and beautiful women. Amity kept her gaze focused outside the carriage on Williamsburg. Clouds hid the moon. Houses slept, but the taverns glowed. Revelers passed in and out of them as the carriage wheeled by. She could barely discern Simon's face across the carriage from where she sat next to her yawning aunt.

"It's a shame we had no time for our game this evening." Simon tossed into the darkness between them.

"You looked as though you enjoyed yourself at cards."

"I did enjoy myself, thank you, Amity."

He didn't mean it. The edge in his voice told her he thought the evening wasted. Well, so did she. Once she heard Will was in the militia, she'd hoped he would have information she could use in her book. Instead, he went on and on about glorious battles he had yet to experience, and all she could think about was brushing up on her nursing skills.

"Oh. You never did make it to your other engagement, did you?"

His tone softened a little. "No, but I have arranged to meet with Dr. Ritter tomorrow morning."

"Is he the gentleman you came to see?"

They pulled up in front of the house before he could answer.

Clementine yawned, made to stand, and plopped back in her seat with another long yawn. "Oh, let me out. I must make for my bed straight away. I don't know when I've been so tired."

Simon obliged them both bowing a good night at the door. Once the door was safely shut behind them, Amity stayed her aunt on the bottom step.

"Who was that woman playing cards with you all night, Aunt?"

Her aunt yawned again, "I thought you knew Sarah Parchment?"

"I do know Mrs. Parchment, but not the other lady."

"Winifred Blackstoke, or stone or something hard like that. She's an odd duck."

"In what way?"

"Apparently she is as much enamored with scientific experiments as your friend Simon Morgan." She yawned until her eyes watered. "I really must go my dear, I've no idea why I'm so tired, maybe all that talk about natural philosophy, but I'm tuckered out."

No wonder there was an edge in his voice. He must really like this new woman who liked science. It made sense. Who would figure that a man could find that singular person, the one woman who alone could make him happy, at a card party at the Peyton's home? She didn't wish to consider why her heart felt pale.

Hopefully, he would still be available to travel. She would have a talk with her aunt first thing in the morning after she spoke with her father again about an interview with the soldiers.

Uncle William's library was dark. Papa must be at the Raleigh with others of the Committee.

Once dressed in her night clothes she sent Lucy on to bed and took a seat at her desk.

Dear Robbie,

I am sure you will be most gratified when you read that I have spent the evening renewing my acquaintance of someone you speak of often in your letters. Will Peyton is as gracious a host, with his mother, as ever he was. He was quite dashing in his new military uniform. It is blue with brass buttons and white cuffs and collar. I've no doubt you will approve of his new look.

He is quite adamant about getting into the fight as soon as ever he can. While it is quite brave, I must say that I understand if it does not make you feel quite the same elation. He complains that there are not enough weapons or powder for his unit to be found, and when it is found, it is likely to be quite dear.

We played backgammon. Of course, I won the match as I usually do.

The most exciting news of me is that I am at last going to the mountains. Aunt Clementine is going to Winchester and Papa has said that I may accompany her. He is going to ask Simon Morgan to accompany us. It's an odd arrangement I must say. It is a very good thing that we know we will not suit one another. We can travel as friends with none of the awkwardness that we would surely feel if we thought there might still be a chance.

Your friend, Amity Archer

~*~

A full moon lit Simon's short walk behind the ordinary. He wound his way past soldiers worse for drink, the dairy, and smokehouse to a quiet spot on the far side of a tree where he wouldn't be spotted. Not the kind of experiment he wanted anyone to see or overhear. And yet he must do it or he'd never know. It was dark enough that any light emanating from the stone would be obvious. He rubbed the back of his neck, fingers sliding into the hair at the nape. Just do it. He looked from right to left and around the back just in case. Two men weaved their way in his direction. The stone lay in his right hand. Just do it. One more look around and he prayed silently for the Lord to tell him if this stone belonged to Him. Simon waited gaze fixed on his hand. Maybe it wasn't good enough to ask quietly. Maybe he needed to say it out loud? "Lord, if this is Your stone, please let it glow once."

Voices boisterous with drink drew close.

Simon closed his fist around the stone and hid it behind his back. After the voices took the shape of their owners and passed, he brought his fist out. Fading light of a trapped lightning bug leaked through his fingers. He opened his fingers to see the moon glow reflected in the clear green stone. Did he see it glow? Was it a trick of the moonlight? He asked again. This time his gaze didn't stray.

Nothing.

Simon marched back to his room. He pulled out his Cruden Concordance, Bible, and extra candles. It would be a long night.

8

Wind ran across open fields, sharpened as it passed between warm dwellings, sliced at Simon's nose and other areas exposed to its cold bite as he trudged beside Parchment through the semi-frozen sandy street toward Charlton's coffee shop.

"And was it worth it?"

"Missing the electricity?" Parchment nodded his assent.

"Yes."

"I played at cards the whole evening with your wife and her unusual friend."

"So I heard."

Simon turned toward his friend.

"Good or bad?"

"Sarah's good opinion of you hasn't altered. In fact, she believes you quite impressed Clementine. And I believe you made a good impression on Mrs. Blackstone."

"Good manners precluded me from doing otherwise."

"Do I detect a note of pique?"

"Perhaps."

Perhaps because he was forced to spend the evening watching another man play his game with

Amity. He wasn't ready to explain himself to his friends. He felt foolish enough about the stone warming his pocket. Yet, since its appearance, his access to Amity had been unprecedented. She'd successfully avoided him ever since she'd decided they wouldn't suit. Hopefully, this meeting would answer his ongoing questions about the stone's murky origins.

The natural philosopher in him required he view the stone with objectivity. He must not allow its possible connection with the present reality cloud his judgment. Never had he struggled quite so much with the requirements of science. He was generally happy when keen observation and repeated experiments demonstrated the true nature of the object of his study.

The lack of wind in Charlton's Coffee House made the large room stuffy and overly warm. February gloom left the room in shadows.

A petit man in a robin-blue coat stepped into their path not two steps past the door. A matching tricorn dangled from the boney fingers of his left hand.

"Mr. Roger White, may I introduce you to my good friend, Simon Morgan?" Parchment gestured toward the man.

Simon nodded a bow allowing his gaze to travel over the plumage of the fellow. From the top of his powdered wig to the gleam of his silver buckles, the man was the very definition of a popinjay.

"Morgan, I understand you have an article I might know something about?" he asked in a dignified whisper.

"Yes, well—"

"Shall we walk?" he waved a boney hand toward the door, "I find it much more private to talk outside."

"I'd prefer to sit in this parlor with a cup of warm coffee if you don't mind. I find it easier to hear indoors instead of fighting a biting wind."

White stiffened. Apparently, he wasn't used to being countered.

"If you insist."

Simon gestured toward their host.

"If you will step this way, gentlemen." Charlton led them to the back of the house.

"Seriously, Mr. White, I do not understand the need for secrecy other than its value. I would not advertise where I kept my valuables, but it is not a secret that I own valuables." Simon sat across a worn planked table from the two men.

White vibrated like an electrified coil.

John sat back in his chair clearly looking forward to the discussion.

"Of course you are right."—White smiled obsequiously darting a quick glance to John—"but there is the matter of public opinion on occultish, or dare I say, magical things."

"There is nothing magical about this stone. At least if there is, I haven't seen it."

White laid his tricorn on the corner of the table leaving his hands free to clasp together on the table. "It's not so much that it is magical, of course, but we don't want people to assume it's magical. Panic will ensue and danger to your life may be the result."

Simon fought the rolling of his eyes. *Really?*

"John—"

"Hear him out, Simon. Roger is an expert on the Horeb stone. If you have it, he will know."

Simon turned back to the little man.

"May I see the stone?"

His hand went to the warm spot in his pocket. Perhaps they were right, if it was the Horeb stone, did he want the whole world to know about it? Did he even want these two to know for certain? Perhaps it was better to keep it hidden. Except then it would continue to be a mystery to him. That would not do. He slipped the flat stone into his hand, his thumb outlining the carved runic writing as he smoothed it between thumb and forefinger. He placed a closed fist on the table between them still deciding. He left the stone and withdrew a hand's breath.

The puffy bags beneath White's eyes receded to reveal large bulbs eager to take in every ounce of light. "May I?" he asked before reaching toward the shining disk.

Simon nodded his assent. John grinned.

"It's either jasper or chalcedony." The man rubbed the stone between his thumb and forefinger. "How did you come by it?"

Simon told the tale of meeting Captain McCabe and his nephew Tom.

All the while Roger gazed at the stone sliding it between his fingers. "Have you noticed any unusual things?"

Trepidation crept up Simon's skin. "What kind of things?"

"Glowing, unusual events?"

Simon hesitated. He thought he'd seen the stone glow, but technically, it didn't count, since he couldn't repeat the experiment. "Not exactly. I've kept it in my pocket since I got it. I have felt it, or at least I thought I felt it, warming my pocket."

Roger nodded his head. "Any events?"

"I'm not sure."

Roger looked up from the stone, his gaze pointed.

"All right. There is a person—" Simon gestured "—and I have wondered if the presence of the stone has brought her back into my life."

Roger looked back down to the stone. "Such things have been known to occur. Artifacts are strange things. We do not understand everything about them. Even now, with all the scientific experimentation and changing thinking about so many things, there are some things, ancient things, that we do not understand." He pushed away from the table still smoothing the stone between his fingers. He held it up to the window light. "Not enough sun." He returned to the table. "If I'm not mistaken it gives a certain feeling of well-being."

Yes. He had felt well since receiving the stone and felt its absence as Roger White held it.

"The writing is ancient Hebrew. I don't know what it says, but I know someone who might be able to help us."

White lay the stone back on the table.

Simon resisted the urge to wipe it clean before putting it back in his pocket.

White angled himself toward John. "We will need to have a meeting before this goes much further."

"So you think it's the stone."

"I think it needs to be investigated further. Others need to see it."

"I will send letters to Fredericksburg and Tappahannock to see what can be arranged."

"That could take a while."

Simon struggled not to laugh at the solemnity of the hushed conversation.

"Gentleman—"

White turned to John. "You haven't told him."

"I thought it best to wait until we knew for sure."

White cleared his throat and turned to face Simon once again.

"Mr. Morgan, we are not permitted to speak of certain things outside of secured areas. We will need to arrange a meeting. You will be invited to bring the stone for evaluation. It may take some days before we can make the arrangements. I trust you will be in Williamsburg?"

Simon felt his eyebrows rise in astonishment. "I cannot say, but John knows where to find me." He wasn't sure if he would attend such a meeting. The nonsense factor was taking on an exponential growth curve.

After the required pleasantries, Simon went out on the street heading toward Anderson's.

"Let's get coffee." John suggested as they dodged the heavy traffic on Duke of Gloucester street.

Simon cast a derisive glance at his companion. "I

could have gotten more information from the boy serving my breakfast."

Anderson showed them to the secluded chamber and sent for coffee.

"It was the first step. You can't get to the others until you see Roger White."

Simon avoided the two tables crammed into the small triangular space. "You're wasting my time. I don't suppose it really matters what the stone is or is not."

"It might. For the stone to show up at this time is important. Who it was given to is also important?"

Simon drew in a deep breath to contain his frustration at the generalities offered by his friend. "I'll ask you this one more time, and if you cannot answer me straight, then we will discuss this no further, and you can tell your friend White not to bother arranging any meetings."

John's eyes widened in surprise. "What do you want to know?"

"I want to know why the stone is so important to Roger White. Who are the people who would want to evaluate the stone? And why? Why is an ancient rock so important?"

John waited while the boy laid the table with coffee and rolls.

Simon grabbed a roll and lathered it with butter.

"The question is whether or not the stone is part of the urim and thummim."

Simon's mind swirled with possibilities. He remembered reading about the urim and thummim in

Scripture, but no particulars came to mind including where to find those passages.

"Refresh my memory—"

"When Moses dressed Aaron in the priestly garments the first time, he slipped the urim and thummim behind the breastplate." John continued. "Some say the breastplate glowed the answer when it was asked a question. I've also heard that the urim glowed when the answer was affirmative and the thummim glowed when the answer was no—"

"So it was binary."

"No one knows for sure. Some say that the individual letters glowed in the breastplate in answer to a question."

"Letters?"

John pulled a small notebook and pencil from his pocket. "The breastplate looked like this." He drew a rectangle with smaller rectangles equally spaced inside the first. "Each of these stones was engraved with the name of one of the twelve tribes of Israel. The thought was that the urim and thummim were engraved with the name of God."

Simon palmed the stone sliding his thumb over the engraved lines. "The name of God."

"Possibly."

"And those were different stones on the breastplate?"

"Nobody knows for sure. Some think it was parchment."

"So what has all this got to do with the Horeb Stone? Does the stone actually exist?"

"The legend says that the stones were given to Moses on Mt. Sinai at the same time he was given the tablets. The stones were carved by God Himself."

"So that is why is shows no wear."

John nodded his agreement.

"And Roger White? I assumed he was with the NTSS."

John glanced over his shoulder. "He is an important man."

Simon gave an eye roll.

"It's who and what he knows."

"So who are the others I'm supposed to meet?"

"Very important men. They will decide the direction this new country will go."

Simon slid back his seat. He'd had enough. "John—"

"Don't be naïve, Simon. Surely you don't buy into all this patriot rot. America may not want a king, but there will be people in charge. They want the stone because they believe it will give them access to God. The ultimate power to rule."

"I'm going for a walk."

"I'll be in touch."

~*~

"Come with me?" Amity's father hadn't bellowed so that was a good sign.

"Yes, please, Papa. It's for my book."

Incredulity hadn't left his face. "Your book."

"I'm having a horrid time describing Williamsburg

at war. I thought visiting the soldiers might help."

"Describing Williamsburg?"

"Yes. From where I sit, it appears the same as it always did. The shops, the taverns, business as usual. But it isn't usual to have soldiers living in tents on the outskirts of town. The threat of a battle breaking out any minute. I mean we feel it, but there is no sign of it."

Papa clicked open his pocket watch. "I shall be leaving in one hour's time."

Elated Amity kissed her father on the cheek. He rested his hands gently on her shoulders gaze pointed into her eyes. "Yes, but you will stay by my side at all times. Tis not a game."

"Yes, Papa."

Precisely one hour later Amity, wrapped in her warmest cloak of indigo wool, sat next to her father in their carriage. Amity rested her hand on the small notebook and pencil tucked into her pocket.

"Sit back, my dear. I cannot see, and I do not wish you to appear over-eager."

Amity slid back quickly. "I'm not over-eager, I'm observing."

"You are your m—" he cleared his throat "—well observe more circumspectly."

Amity grinned. "Mama is worse than I am when it comes to being excited."

His face softened in affection. "She is..." His far-away look focused back on Amity. "But she would not like you visiting soldiers, so don't forget her temper."

Amity straightened. Sobering thought, Mama's temper.

The sandy, water-logged roads slowed their passage. Once past William and Mary the camp came into full view. Rows and rows of tents in whites and tans of sailcloth and duck formed a small village of mud streets.

"Is no one in charge here?"

"Patrick Henry. Although, there has been some news." The coach stopped at the first corner on the edge of the camp.

Her father climbed down from the coach and immediately turned to the group of officers extending their greetings. Amity stepped over a puddle at the bottom of the carriage steps only to slip on a paper-thin sheet of ice covering a cold pudding of mud that oozed up the sides of her boots.

A man in regimentals appeared at her elbow with a steadying hand as she righted herself.

"Careful," a familiar voice said.

She looked up into the eyes of Will Peyton. "Thank you."

"Peyton, is it?" Her father extended a hand.

Will straightened as he took the offered hand. "Yes sir."

Perfect timing. Will would surely distract her father, which should give her a chance to really visit the camp. Amity took a quiet step away from her father.

"Has Colonel Henry visited the camp today?" Papa filled the space Amity vacated.

"No, sir, but he has extended an invitation for his officers to attend dinner with him this evening at the

Raleigh." Will's inclusion in the party was evident in his increased stature. Beyond them, a red-nosed soldier, wiping nose-drips on his sleeve, sat on a three-legged stool sharpening a knife. He stilled at the mention of Henry's name and looked in their direction. Meeting Amity's gaze, he slowly resumed the scratch of his blade across the stone.

"You must be relieved that Clinton sailed south?"

Across from the knife soldier, a curly haired woman emerged from a tent carrying a kettle in one hand and a small sack in another. She tipped her head toward the knife-soldier and walked quickly toward the center of camp.

"Well..."

9

Amity didn't hear the rest of the conversation. Stepping around muddy ruts she followed the tidy, brown-haired woman past tents sodden with yesterday's rain to a fire pit ringed with soldiers and a couple of women.

The woman she followed placed her kettle on the ground next to the fire. "Who are ye with then?"

Amity's cold face flamed. "I beg your pardon?"

"Who's your man?"

"I haven't got one." That got everyone's attention. One soldier stood.

"Well, then, ye can be off."

"I meant no harm. I didn't plan to stay."

"What're ye doing here?" A younger woman dressed in an oversized brown frock coat stepped next to the woman she'd followed.

"I'm here with my father. He has business with Major Peyton."

"So you're along for the tea are ye?" The woman she'd followed laughed.

The others twittered.

"No—I." Amity twisted her fingers inside her warm muff. In one glance, she took in the woman's splitting fingertips. "I wanted to come and—"

A cold breeze troubled brown curly wisps surrounding brown eyes tenderized by grief. "Good men died at Norfolk."

Amity's heart filled her chest. *I shouldn't have come.*

The woman remained, her chapped features frozen.

Amity squared her stance. "I came because I want to tell the story."

"Ain't no story. It is the truth." The younger woman spat.

"It is the truth I wish to tell. To record. So that your children, my children, will know what happened."

The younger woman grabbed hold of the curly haired woman's arm. "Come on, Mary. Her kinds got no time for the likes of us."

"Ye're goin'ta print it then?"

Amity's conviction came from a solid place of surety deep inside herself that she didn't know existed. She would write the accounts, and she would have them printed. "Yes."

"Like a book."

"Yes. It will be a book." Her concept of the book morphed rapidly. What it would be hadn't taken shape yet, but it would be different from the animal stories she crafted for her siblings.

Mary wrenched her arm from her companion's and pointed Amity to an empty stool. "I'll tell ye about my Daniel if ye'll print it. His parents would love that and so will my son." She looked pointedly at the group. "And *me*."

Mary placed her kettle on the hook over the fire and gave it a stir before sitting next to her. Amity could just see her father's coat sleeve from her spot next to the fire.

Mary described how Daniel and his brother, Jonathan, decided to join the army. How they followed Woodford to Norfolk. Fighting Captain Squire at Hampton. Crossing the James River in fishing boats while evading the captain. Boldly standing against Dunmore and his fleet while they threatened the inhabitants of Norfolk.

Amity's heart quickened. A vision of Simon against the silhouettes of burning warehouses avoiding falling planks running alongside Daniel filled her mind. Simon leading his men in a charge against the invading British while safeguarding women and children still fleeing for their lives into the surrounding countryside. Daniel died of a British bullet on Church Street. Her vision stopped short of tears when she saw a bloodied Simon breathing his last on a flame-lit street.

"How will you get home?" he asked.

"Jonathan will take me and Danny back home when his enlistment is up next month. If he lasts that long."

"Is he injured?"

"No. But if the rumors are right, and Colonel Henry isn't made general, he won't stay."

"Do they care so much for Colonel Henry?"

Mary stood and curtseyed. "Major Peyton."

Will acknowledged Mary with a slight nod. "Miss

Archer, your father has been worried."

"Peyton."

Will swung around.

A glow of relief calmed Amity. A broad grin spread across her face before she could check herself. "Simon." Not bloody. Breathing. Full of air, in fact.

"I have been here with Miss Archer, Peyton. There is nothing to fear."

Amity stepped across the space between them and took Simon's arm.

"Morgan. Didn't know you were here." Her father boomed into the group.

"Reed. Good to see you. I was out for a walk and chanced across Amity listening to a riveting account of the battle of Norfolk."

"Indeed." Papa gave Mary a once over.

Amity introduced Mary Cook to her father.

"May I come back to see you?" Amity asked.

"If you like, miss."

"I should. I haven't taken any notes, and I do wish to get it right."

Mary bobbed a short curtsy. Amity did the same, and Mary's eyes widened. "Not between friends," she whispered.

The muddy path between the tents was not quite wide enough for Amity to take Simon's offered arm, so she followed her father with Simon and Will close behind.

"Nice to see you again, Miss Archer. Perhaps I shall see you yet again before you return home." Will ventured once they'd reached the carriage.

"Perhaps you will, Mr. Peyton." Amity turned from him to face the carriage.

Simon offered his hand as she placed her foot on the first step. "I understand you will be attending Andersons' ball tonight."

"Yes, I believe my father will attend us this evening."

"Will you save me a dance?"

I'll save all of them if it will keep the suitors away. "I'd be delighted."

He handed her up into the coach. The clanging rustle of the camp quieted behind the doors of the carriage.

"I specifically required you to stay by my side while I visited the camp."

"I know, Papa, but standing there listening to you talk to Will Peyton is no different than me talking to him at the card party a few nights ago." They pulled away from the camp. "I could see you from where I sat."

"The point is I could not see you."

"Yes. Papa."

"You may not go there again."

"But—"

"Never again."

She knew the tone.

He would not change his mind.

But Mary Cook could come out of the camp. She would send a note inviting her to tea. She would probably laugh at that. She sat back against the seat and let her mind fill with the images Mary had painted. There was much to record before she dressed for the ball that evening. She didn't have time to examine why Simon had filled her head as Mary described her ordeal.

Amity had filled ten pages of her journal by the time Lucy came to help her dress for Anderson ball. Emotionally drained, she let Lucy choose her dress. White cotton printed with crimson birds and flowers. Wigs no longer being the fashion since the start of hostilities, white ribbons adorned her hair.

A giddy thrill vibrated through Amity as she gazed in Andersons' window. Dancers bobbed and swirled to the music provided by the band in a corner of the room she couldn't see from the street. She hoped a few soldiers would be present at tonight's ball, so she could ask about the action they'd seen so far. Mary's account was vivid enough to evoke visions of Simon, but it was only one version. It would make a very short and lopsided book. She needed more material. She supposed it would depend on whether or not the men had the funds. She and her aunt attended for free, women always did at these things, while men had to pay.

Mr. Anderson bowed before her aunt. "Mrs. Foster, so glad you could attend this evening."

Aunt Clementine preened in her indigo gown. Even her father, despite being fifty-five on his last birthday, looked dashing in his full dress of hunter green. Across the street in the candle glow of the Raleigh soldiers laughed.

Amity gestured toward the group. "It must be

Colonel Henry."

"Yes, that is him. Front and center."

"I wonder why he is out tonight. The rumor I heard was that he did not receive what he requested from Congress."

"You heard correctly. He has been given and *turned down* command of the First Virginia Regiment. He's leaving tomorrow."

"Turned it down?"

"He wanted to be commander and chief."

At once enveloped in the warmth and light of the room Amity scanned to see if she knew anyone. She missed Robbie at once. How hard it was not to have a confidant when so many incredible things were happening.

Simon bounced into view. He led Mrs. Blackstone expertly through a turn in the set.

Amity's buoyancy flattened.

Robbie never said a bad thing about anyone. She could help Amity find something good to think about the black-haired, porcelain doll that was Winifred Blackstone. More importantly, how had she forgotten that Simon was smitten and would not likely be available to keep unwanted suitors away? Obviously, his asking her to dance this evening was only to mask his attentions to Mrs. Blackstone. One didn't dance too often with one's intended until she was formally one's intended. It's not as though Amity cared anyway. How often had she told herself they wouldn't suit? She should be grateful to him for taking the burden of respectability off her shoulders. "Would you care for some punch, Aunt?"

"Not yet, child. We've only just arrived. I do not see our friend Mr. Peyton among the set."

"I believe he is with Colonel Henry tonight."

"More's the pity," Clementine muttered.

Grateful for small mercies, Amity drifted behind Clementine as she sought a chair. Her father worked his way toward a group of men standing in the far corner of the room by the bar.

"At least I see your Mr. Morgan." Clementine arranged her skirts around knees that sat at a little higher angle when she was in small chairs. She slipped her crossed ankles to one side. She looked uncomfortable. No wonder Uncle William finally made chairs for them both.

"You misunderstand Aunt. Simon is an old family friend."

Clementine was not convinced.

"I believe she—" Amity indicated Mrs. Blackstone "—is much more to his liking. She is bookish like him."

Clementine waved her hand. "Enough. You don't know what you are talking about."

The set ended, and as Simon led Mrs. Blackstone to the punch table near the entrance, one of her father's friends presented himself.

"Miss Archer, would you do me the honor?"

Amity knew his wife and daughters; there was no danger from this man. "I'd be delighted Mr. Lewis."

Following the set, another of her father's friends arrived to escort her to the floor. She wondered if he was slipping them each a coin. After the third set,

Amity pleaded exhaustion and headed for her aunt.

"Your father is taking me home."

"Are you not well? I'll get our things."

Clementine caught her hand before she could move. "He has already gone to get them. You may stay. Mr. Morgan can bring you home."

"Aunt."

"He has your father's blessing."

Amity paled. "Blessing for what?"

"Did your father not ask him to escort you as he would his own sister?"

"Yes, of course, but I can be ready to leave with you and Papa. There is nothing to keep me here."

"Nothing?" Simon appeared at her side. "I believe you promised me a dance."

"So I did—"

"Very good to see you, Mr. Morgan." Clementine bestowed on Simon the same beam of graciousness she'd given to Mr. Anderson upon their arrival. "Reed will take me home. I trust you may escort our girl home when this merriment is concluded?"

"Indeed I shall."

"What shall you do, Mr. Morgan?" Mrs. Blackstone asked.

If she looked like porcelain at a distance, up close she was nearly flawless. Amity would have to take some time later to determine why she was not happy for him. She supplied the required bob when the introductions came around to her.

The fiddler drew his bow across the strings.

"Amity?" Simon offered his hand.

She placed her hand in his.

"Mrs. Blackstone, may I present my dear friend, Mr. Lewis." Papa bellowed.

Amity retreated to the dance floor hiding a smile.

She stood across from Simon and slipped back to the first dance they'd shared. Oh, how her heart thrilled when he'd offered his hand. Hazel eyes sparkling as they did now, changing color in the candlelight. Chestnut hair pulled into a curlew at his neck. Broader now, he filled his suit with a manly bearing that was missing when last they'd danced. He was all man now with the same open smile that caused her lungs to deflate.

Turning under his arm brought her close enough to smell the pine soap he always used. Images of walking with him in the gloaming, golden lights twinkling out of windows, speaking of homey things— none of that. *He belongs to Mrs. Blackstone.* Good thing she knew they would never suit or she'd be in big trouble. The set finished in a flourish and not too soon for her ragged emotions. Distance. That's what she needed. Punch.

"That was rigorous set. Would you care for a drink?"

Groaning out loud was not anymore polite than 'I need some distance to figure out what your presence is doing to me' so she settled on, "Yes, I would, thank you."

Mrs. Blackstone occupied the chair vacated by Aunt Clementine.

Amity chose to follow Simon to the refreshments.

The line for a cool drink angled from the stairs toward the street entrance. Amity took her place next to Simon amidst the few gathered in the vestibule. Through the farthest window, which gave a mere slice of a glance into the street, she gleaned movement. She moved to the doorway. From the door, she saw them come. Like a snowball gathering mass, soldiers rolled down the street.

Glass shattered. Dance music played behind her. The mob kept coming. Men hastily pulled on coats, and stood on porches, wives, and children close behind.

"What do you think they want?" Simon's voice tickled her ear. A crowd formed behind them jostling for a look.

"I'm not sure, but I'll find out." Amity stepped off the porch and entered the crowd. She pushed her way toward the center. Soldiers, raising fists and shouting to be released, moved out of her way at a slight nudge. "What's it about?" She asked the first soldier.

The man turned toward her. "Who are you then?" The man grabbed her waist sliding his hands higher. "Ain't you fancy?"

Her voice deserted her. She dug her heels in to push away but found no purchase in the muddy sand. She balled both fists and hit him in the ear.

"Hey!" He released her and took a step back.

Amity retreated into a wall. "Don't you dare touch me."

The man's eyes widened, and he put up his hands.

Another pair of hands landed on her shoulders.

Without a blink, she spun around and swung her fist. Simon caught the blow in his much larger hand.

"Amity?"

"That man—" She turned to point to the man, but he was gone.

A whistle shot through the crowd.

Simon rested hands on her shoulders. Chest heaving, Amity stepped back into his protection.

The soldiers stilled and waited.

"Gentleman," Patrick Henry's voice rang through the street. "I have heard your requests to be released from your enlistments. Let us go back to camp to discuss it, shall we? Business of this important a nature should not be discussed on our public streets. I order you back to your camp. I shall be with you shortly."

"Now. Amity." Simon released her shoulders and grabbed her hand. He let her go only after he'd gotten her back to Anderson's. "Do not go outside." He ordered before marching off.

The soldiers retreated from the door.

"That was very foolish of you, Miss Archer. You could have been killed or worse." Mrs. Blackstone called her attention back to the people standing around her in the vestibule.

Anger blazed. Amity crossed her arms. "Nonsense. I was very safe among the soldiers of our country."

A sardonic look pinched Mrs. Blackstone's face. "Suit yourself, but you should be careful out there among unsupervised men. Dressed as you are what do you think they will take you for? Certainly not a fine lady. They will treat you as they think you are."

Amity tugged at her stomacher, rising bile burned her throat. Of course, that is what the soldier would have thought.

Where was that coach?

~*~

Simon held Amity's hand across the yard to the carriage and handed her in. He took deep even breaths. This was not like dealing with Hester. Hester knew he loved her. Hester knew his authority. He'd had occasion to lay down the law. She yelled and carried on until they could come to some agreement. He had no authority over Amity. She could walk away convinced once again that they wouldn't suit. Maybe she was right. The tension hadn't left his body from finding her among the troops earlier in the day before he lost her in the mob. "Tell me that somehow you were pushed off those steps. That you did not deliberately walk into that mob of soldiers."

She said nothing, face turned toward the window.

"Your father will ask me..."

"I stepped down."

He slapped his hands on his knees and swallowed an expletive. "How will I explain that you were accosted in a mob of soldiers because I didn't prevent you from taking off?"

"I didn't think—"

"That much would be obvious to a deluded person."

"Simon."

"Are you deluded?"

"No. I am writing a book."

He sat back and folded his arms. "You are writing a book." Of course, he knew she wrote tales for her siblings. He'd heard they were quite good, but this was the first he'd heard anything like this.

"Yes."

"I didn't think you wrote about those kinds of animals."

"It's not a child's book."

"Go on."

"I would love to, but we have arrived. I hope you don't have to tell Papa about this evening, but if you do, then I shall deal with the consequences. But I am not sorry."

10

"Good evening, Miss Amity."

Amity gave Lucy her cloak and muff.

"Mr. Morgan, Mr. Archer asked if you would please meet with him in Mr. William's book room."

"Yes, of course."

"Lucy, if anyone asks, I'll be in my room preparing for bed." Amity curtsied. "Thank you for escorting me home, Simon. I had a lovely time."

He bowed rather than show the anger that still shook him by taking her hand.

Simon arrived at the study door.

"I thought you wanted to get out of town, Clementine."

"Have you spoken to Mr. Morgan about escorting us to Winchester?"

"If I do so this evening will you make your arrangements?"

"Yes."

Simon stepped into the doorway.

Clementine stood. "The man himself."

"Simon, I have a very great favor to ask of you."

"You want me to escort your daughter and her aunt to Winchester?"

Reed's features stilled.

"I heard you as I walked down the hall."

Reed relaxed. "Clementine is anxious to get out of town. Amity has always wanted to see the mountains—"

"I have old friends in Winchester." Clementine continued, "it is past time I went to see them. The fighting seems to have quieted in that part of the world, at least for now."

The idea of taking Amity and her aunt out of town was too good to be true. There must be some kind of catch somewhere. He put his hand in his pocket and cupped the stone.

"I believe I will have time to take them, Reed, provided it is not to be an extended stay."

"We should be gone a month, no longer than six weeks, depending on the weather, of course."

"Of course."

Lists appeared in Simon's mind. A letter to his steward and foreman. He would send for Jax.

"Not a bad time of year for such a trip. Planting won't start for at least that long."

"Mr. Morgan, I don't know how I can thank you." Clementine took one of his hands in both of hers. "I'll be off to bed now. Can you be ready in two days?"

"I believe I can. I will make some arrangements and send word to confirm when I have completed my preparations."

Clementine swept from the room.

Reed poured them each a drink. "Sit down, son. I've a question to ask you before you embark on this journey."

They sat across from each other in front of the small fire. Reed spoke so softly Simon wasn't sure he heard him.

"Did you ask me if I'm prepared to marry your daughter if she is compromised on this trip?"

"Yes. Keep your voice down, I've no wish for the entire house to know our business."

"Have you asked Amity this question?"

Reed nodded his affirmation and took another sip of the amber liquid.

"And she said yes?" Simon's spirit shot like a star across the sky.

"Yes, she did. Of course she doesn't think anything like that can happen to her."

His spirit dropped to its usual place. "Is that why she was in the soldier's camp today?"

"She's researching a book. And mind you, she writes well, but she doesn't understand the world. She thinks she can wander all over God's earth as if she's back home."

Images of Amity on a stool in the camp in the midst of the mob of soldiers came to his mind. "I noticed."

"I've protected her for too long."

A picture of Field's wife, Delany, trapped under a smuggler replaced Amity in an instant.

"What else are we to do with girls, Reed? True evil can ruin them."

"True evil can ruin anyone."

"Yes, but we're stronger."

"Sometimes."

Simon filled his lungs. He'd had about enough arguing with Archers for one day. "Physically we are stronger than women."

"Yes, but are we as resilient? I've seen my wife smile after two solid days of ungodly caterwauling of one of her children."

Simon offered his glass in salute. "That's not evil."

"No, but it is strength."

Simon let his eyes glaze over at the flames dancing in the grate.

"It is past time that she grew up and learned something of the world."

Outrage turned Simon to Reed. "You'll let her put herself at risk?"

"No. That's what you are for. I expect you to keep her safe from herself and others."

"I don't have the authority to do that."

"You did a fine job today at the camp." Reed sipped. "Later in the mob."

"You heard about that?"

"A friend sent a message just before you arrived. You handled it as I would have. Am I happy about it? No. But Amity will put herself in danger until she learns some sense. Hopefully, this trip will teach her something."

"Reed. I don't think—"

"You're not fooling me, son. I've seen the way you look at my daughter. The way you looked at me when you thought I didn't care enough to escort her to an ordinary."

Reed had him there. Simon glanced down at the

fire reflected in his glass. "She told me once that she didn't think we would suit."

"She said that, did she?" Reed chuckled. "Her mother told me the same thing."

"I respected her wishes and stayed away."

"How old was she?" Simon asked.

"Seventeen."

"How old was Mrs. Archer when you married?"

"Eighteen. Look Simon, it's hard for a girl to see a man clearly when she is so young. She's not allowed to be with you alone. Even chaperoned, she can only spend a few minutes at a time."

"What changed Mrs. Archer's mind about you?"

"I fixed a situation she thought was of my making. More importantly she needed to see that I was not my father."

"I'm confident Amity doesn't think I'm anything like you, sir."

"It doesn't matter what bothered her then. This is your chance to change her mind about you now."

"I have your blessing then?"

Reed nodded. "So what will you do about it?"

"I guess I'm going to Winchester."

~*~

A shutter banged against her window and knocked Amity right out of a deep sleep. Tendrils of a dream gently pulled her back in. Why was it so bright in her room?

Lucy rushed to the window to fasten the shutter

back in place. "Miss Amity. That wind is howlin'" The blast of cold air whipped the pages of Amity's journal and sent her carefully penned note to Mary to the floor. Amity jumped out of bed. "What time is it?"

"Half past nine. I figured as you was out so late you need your rest."

"Have this note taken to Mrs. Mary Cook. She is serving in the Army camp the other side of the college."

"Yes, miss."

"And hurry. I hope to see Mary for tea today."

Amity chose her warmest brown woolen petticoat and mantua. Making her way down to breakfast she thanked the Lord for a day free of plans. She would have plenty of time to revise what she'd written and work on further questions for Mary.

"Good morning, sleepy head." Clementine folded her copy of Purdy's Virginia Gazette. "I have news."

"What news?"

"Get your breakfast."

Amity chose a plate from the sideboard and filled it with ham and bread.

"Your father has spoken to your Mr. Morgan."

Amity placed a hand on her stomach to keep it from rolling. She'd hoped Simon wouldn't tell Papa about the mob. She took a quiet, deep breath and squared her shoulders. She meant what she said. She wasn't sorry. "He is not *my* Mr. Morgan. You heard Papa, if he was interested in me, he would have offered years ago."

"Do you want to hear the news or not?"

Amity's face warmed. "Of course."

Clementine passed the tea.

"Mr. Morgan agreed to escort us to Winchester. We leave in two days' time."

"You are not jesting, are you, Aunt?"

"Certainly not." Clementine stirred her tea…a conspiratorial twinkle lit her blue eyes. "I never jest about adventure."

Amity clasped her hands together and let the biggest smile she was capable of erupt across her face. "I cannot believe it! You are absolutely sure?"

"You may ask your father when you see him if you don't believe me."

"I am sorry. If you knew how I've longed to see something beyond fifty miles from home." She sighed. "All the places I've read about."

"Well, my dear. Winchester is not so grand a place, but we *shall* see it." Clementine slipped back behind her paper.

Amity didn't taste her breakfast as her mind raced through the possibilities of their trip. They would have to take the King's Highway through Fredericksburg then west toward Winchester. Robbie had provided all the details during her last visit. Perhaps Clementine was right; Winchester may be underwhelming, but this was only the beginning of her travels. She would prove that a woman could travel on her own safely. Then the only limit was her imagination. Her dreams took full flight thinking of trips to cool cliff breezes all the way to the desert heat of Egypt.

Amity plunged into packing. She was up to her

elbows in her trunk when Lucy announced Mary's arrival. She took a moment to look in the glass to straighten her hair before grabbing ink and paper.

Mary stood before Clementine with a blond-haired bundle suspended on her hip.

"He is two this past week," Mary said as Amity entered the parlor.

Amity put her quill and ink on a side table.

"This must be Danny."

"Yes, miss."

Danny tucked his head into Mary's shoulder. "I hope ye don't mind. I couldn't leave him."

"Don't give it another thought," Clementine said. "It's good to see a baby." She stuck a finger toward Danny's belly. The toddler smiled from his mother's shoulder. "I haven't seen my grandchildren since Christmas."

"He makes me wish to see my younger brothers." Amity smiled at the little boy.

Tense lines in Mary's face relaxed into a smile at their welcome.

"I invited Mary to tea so she could finish telling me about her ordeal at Norfolk."

"You were at Norfolk?" Momentarily distracted from the child, Clementine searched her face.

"My husband fought. I was in camp."

"Of course." Clementine reached for Danny. "Will he come to me?"

Danny leaned his body over, and Clementine scooped him up. "Would you like to find some toys?" Clementine raised her eyebrows at Mary. Mary nodded her approval. Clementine took him into a room across the hall.

"My friend Jane—you met her yesterday—wanted to come. I told her ye can't just invite y'self to tea at someone's house. But I did say I would ask if ye wanted to talk to her too."

"Was she—"

"The one with no manners? Yes." Mary glanced quickly around the room. The crimson papered walls and settees must look opulent to someone living in a tent. "She's not so bad once you get to know her. She can be hard to get to know."

Amity gestured to her new friend. "Please sit down and be comfortable."

Mary sat on the edge of a cream-colored settee. "I laughed when I read ye note inviting me to tea."

"I thought you might."

Danny toddled in carrying a ball on a stick.

Clementine followed carrying a small box of toys.

"These belong to my grandchildren." She placed the box near Mary. "I shall see about some refreshment."

"I thought I saw you in the crowd last night."

Mary shook her head. "I was home with Danny. Jonathan vowed he'd leave if Colonel Henry wasn't...reinstated, or whatever the word is."

"He didn't leave without you?"

"No. Colonel Henry spent the entire night in the camp. Going from fire to fire. When he was done, they was settled down. I reckon they'll stay and do their duty when all's said and done."

"You don't mind?" Amity retrieved her writing implements. "I'll never remember all of this if I don't take some notes."

"You go right ahead." Mary slipped off the chair onto the floor with Danny.

"However do you sit down there with all your petticoats and things?"

"We'd catch fire for sure if we wore as much as proper ladies. Not that we ain't proper, ye understand." She sat up a little straighter and looked Amity in the eye. "I work for the Army. General Washington pays me for my work."

"So you are a patriot, Mary."

Mary grinned. "Yes, miss. I am that."

"Would you have tried to go to the Army if you hadn't followed your husband?"

"You mean like them stories? I haven't met any of them women that's pretending to be men so they can fight. I don't think I'd've had the gumption for that."

"But you followed Daniel."

"It's different, isn't it? Daniel was my husband. Where else would I want to be?"

"What happened to your home?"

Puzzlement crossed her features.

"Don't you have a home of your own to go back to when this is over?"

"No. Daniel and I lived on his parents' farm before the Army. We planned to go back there and build a house not far..." Tears spilled down her cold-reddened cheeks. She teased a blonde curl from Danny as he chewed on a block.

Clementine sailed into the room followed by Matilda carrying a tea tray. "May I give Danny a cookie?"

Mary wiped her face with a handkerchief while nodding her consent.

"It's warmer here by the fire, if you would like to move closer." Clementine suggested.

"I believe I'm thawing out right here. I might leave a puddle by the time I'm through."

Clementine and Amity both laughed.

"My dear, you are welcome in my home anytime," Clementine said.

As the afternoon faded into evening, Mary told her story of following her husband to the Army.

Amity took copious notes. This time when Mary told of fighting with Captain Squire at Hampton, Amity did not see Simon; she saw Danny.

"Will you come tomorrow?" Amity asked when Mary stood to take her leave.

"If ye wish it. Do ye still want to see Jane?"

Amity nodded. The more women and soldiers she could interview the better for the book that was taking shape in her mind.

Mary and Danny left their home with cheerful goodbyes and walked down the street toward the camp.

"So tell me about this book you propose to write." Clementine smiled when Amity returned to the parlor.

The wonder of the task filled her heart. The worry that she was naive or worse, full of hubris, twisted her stomach. "I'm not sure what the final outcome will be, but I want to tell the story of this time."

Clementine gestured for her to continue.

"I have read so many adventures of people traveling around the world. But they leave out all the important elements. Like how people live in different parts of the world. I want to write that."

"Like the women serving in the Army."

"Exactly. I never thought of women being there, fighting alongside their men and brothers."

"I am continually astounded by how much of our lives remain untouched by the war we are actively fighting. Life goes on, planting, dancing, marrying…"

"After spending time with Mary I'm not sure I can. How can I do justice to her sacrifice?"

"If you don't write it, who will?"

Her stomach eased. "I hadn't thought of it like that."

"A worthy endeavor. You write it, I'll see to it that it's printed."

11

A stiff gale pebbled Simon with sandy debris as he dodged traffic across Duke of Gloucester Street to the Raleigh Tavern.

"Mr. Morgan?" A short, square man approached dressed in a sober brown frock coat, plain vest, and breeches.

"Dr. Ritter?"

"Yes."

Simon bowed. "It is an honor, sir."

"The honor is mine."

"I cannot thank you enough for agreeing to meet with me. I have been reading your papers since I was in the schoolroom." Simon smiled.

Ritter flushed pink and a twinkle lit his blue eyes. "Time is an interesting thing, is it not? Perhaps we should commence our business together before I hit my dotage, eh?" He spun toward the stairs. "I've set up in my room. Less likely to be disturbed. Come with me."

Simon followed the man up a narrow set of stairs. On a rectangular pine table under the only window in the small room sat a wooden box filled with bottles connected at the top by thin brass rods. To its left stood an apparatus that reminded Simon of his mother's spinning wheel albeit turned on its side.

At the top of this electricity-producing machine perched a glass sphere. Three needles ascended from the globe to converge into one at the top. This primary needle was connected via a thin wire to the bottles in the box.

To the right of the box on the table sat a sealed, three-foot glass tube. The bottom hosted a brass disk, midway down the tube was another brass disk.

"Dr. Watson's experiment, is it?"

A young boy emerged from Ritter's enthusiasm. "You know it?"

"Only what Priestly wrote about it. I have yet to see it performed."

"It's more impressive in the dark, but as it is day, we shall have to do what we can." He drew the curtain. Ritter applied himself to link the electrostatic machine with the battery. "Are you ready?"

Simon indicated that he was indeed ready.

Ritter turned the crank on the machine. After a few turns a spark leapt across the line to the glass bottles.

"They charge all at once you see." Ritter waved over the box. "Now, watch this." He connected the battery to the glass tube.

Instantly electric fire arced between the two brass plates in the glass tube, causing it to glow. It lasted a few seconds.

"Can you do it again?"

"Of course."

Dr. Ritter stepped through the same procedures again with the same result.

"How can we make it last longer?"

"Good question, my boy."

"It needs a constant supply of electricity."

"And uninterrupted flow—" He counted on his fingers "—and we may need a way to contain the heat. Those plates are not hot, but this is a very short experiment. Suppose we wanted to keep the light on as long as we burn a candle?"

The answer to brighter, sustainable light dangled just out of grasp, but it wouldn't be long.

"Is there any way that I may assist you?"

"I assume you mean besides financial assistance." Simon nodded his agreement, although he wasn't averse to that aspect either. "Perhaps there is. Shall I write to you of my next steps?"

"Yes, sir. I should be delighted to help in any way I can." Simon shook the man's hand and prepared to leave when he remembered the stone. "Dr. Ritter. Might I ask you a favor?"

"Depends on what it is."

"I have recently acquired an artifact. I would like to understand its properties."

"You would like to test it on my machine?"

"Yes."

"All it will tell you is whether it conducts electricity or not."

"I know, but it's a rather unusual thing."

"Let's see it."

Simon handed him the stone.

"Is this what I think it is? The Horeb Stone?"

"You know of it?"

Dr. Ritter held it up to the light. "I would be surprised at any educated man not being aware of the stone." He handed it back to Simon. "How came you by it?"

Simon told the tale of Captain McCabe's nephew and how he bought the stone.

"Have you talked to God?"

"What?"

"You should review your Scriptures, my boy. King David inquired of the urim and thummim before he fought the Philistines."

Simon had read the references John had given him, but he'd missed these.

"If this is the urim, I'm not sure it will work for you."

"Why?"

"Because you are not the high priest of Israel."

Simon glanced down at the stone in his hand. "I think I saw it glow."

The blue eyes widened in surprise, curiosity in their depths. "So you want to know if it conducts electricity."

"Yes."

"It could ruin any magic associated with it."

"If it's of God nothing we do will destroy it."

"Moses destroyed the first tablets."

Simon paused. "Yes, but the urim and thummim were not supposed to be magic, more a conduit of information."

The old man nodded and turned toward his equipment. He waved to the table. "Be my guest."

Simon laid the stone on the table in front of the glass tube on top of the wire that would have connected to the tube.

Dr. Ritter turned the crank on the electrostatic machine. An arc of electric fire passed to the battery through the connecting rod to the stone.

The stone jumped and the writing in the center lit with a golden fire that blazed bright enough to stain Simon's eyes with its brilliance. "Did you see that?"

Dr. Ritter shook his head up and down.

"What does it mean?"

Dr. Ritter plopped down in the only chair in the room. "Did it look like what you saw before?"

"No. It was much brighter. What I saw before looked like a lightning bug which faded away."

"There could be gold or some other mineral catching the fire, but I didn't see any trace of it in the writing. And it didn't fire anywhere else...did it?"

"Let's do it again."

Dr. Ritter took his place by the crank. The result was the same.

"By our observation it is possible that your rock, for it is a rock, contains some mineral like gold or silver that conducts electricity."

Simon had to agree. In other experiments, he'd seen gold lettering burn when electricity was applied to a leather book with an embossed gold title. "But it does not explain why it was confined to the writing alone."

The twinkle was back in the blue eyes. "Whatever you do, I would take very good care of that rock."

"You can believe I will, sir."

"I shall write to you of my experiments, and you let me know what you find out. I think I shall be reading your papers before too long."

Maybe. As Simon put the stone back in his pocket, he was pretty confident he'd be keeping this discovery to himself.

Later that night in his bed Simon alternated between wondering how long the lone window in his room would remain intact in the hurricane wind that cracked tree limbs and pelted debris against the roof, and the bewildering results of his electrical experiment with the stone.

The stone conducted electricity but only in the letters in the center. That might be significant if he knew what the letters meant. Right now, he didn't know anything. Tomorrow he would set out a list of questions and start asking to see what kind of response he would get from the stone.

~*~

The next day a windblown pair with Danny in tow arrived on the doorstep. Clementine opened the door herself. "Good afternoon, Danny," she cooed.

Danny leaned his body forward for Clementine to take him. She placed him on her hip and slipped away talking of cookies as big as his hand.

"Good afternoon, Mary." Amity swung open the door. "And you must be Jane. Please come in..."

Mary stepped with confidence, her friend less so.

"I do hope you will make yourself at home, Jane." Amity waved toward the room. "Please take a seat."

Jane kept her eyes down. She sat ramrod straight in the smallest chair in the room.

"I'm glad you decided to come." Amity offered to the downcast Jane.

"Thank ye for inviting us. Danny has talked of little but cookies since we came away."

"Yes." Jane raised her gaze to take in the room. "Thank ye for inviting me."

"I understand you would like to tell me your story."

"It ain't a story. It's the truth." Jane stated the fact with little of the emotion she'd spat in their last encounter.

"I do apologize. I meant the account. You would like for me to record your accounting of what you have seen."

"Yes. I'll buy a subscription, and when it's ready ye can send it along."

"I shall be happy to send you a copy."

"I'll pay me own way." She stuffed a hand down into the folds of her skirts and produced a shilling.

"I'm not yet prepared to take your money."

"How will I know you'll send me the book?"

"Jane!" Mary placed a hand on her friend's arm. "Amity's got nothing to gain from telling our accounts. She will send the book when it's finished."

"I give you my word." Amity assured them.

"How will you find me?"

"Why not tell me where you live. Once it's

printed, I will send your copy to your home. It will be waiting for you when you get there."

Jane returned the coin to its hiding place deep in the folds of her brown homespun gown.

Amity made careful notes of Jane's direction in North Carolina and Mary's in Winchester.

"Winchester? My aunt has an old friend there. She and I will be leaving for Winchester in the next couple of days."

"What is the friend's name? Maybe I know the family."

"Jedidiah Eberly. Apparently, he and my Uncle William were great friends."

Danny ran into the room and bounced into his mother's lap.

Clementine carried a tea tray followed by Lucy with a tray of cakes. The repast filled the small tea table. "And Ann was my dearest friend. She died last year." Clementine finished.

"So you are from Winchester, Mary?"

"Yes, Mrs. Foster. My husband's family owns a large farm there."

"Then perhaps we will see you again there."

"Perhaps you might. Jonathan, my husband's brother, informed me that his enlistment is up, and we will be leaving for home by the end of the week."

Jane's upturned smile turned into a resigned grimace. "It's sudden, is it not? I thought he wouldn't be released until next month."

"Yes, we had thought so ourselves, but planting will be starting soon, and if we start out now, we will be home in plenty of time." Mary blinked back the droplets forming at the corners of her eyes. She squeezed her little boy. "It will be good to be home. Won't it, Danny?"

He handed her a slobbery stick.

"I do hope we shall see you there."

Clementine offered Jane a cup of tea. "Where do you call home, Jane?"

A slight tremor jittered the cup on the saucer until Jane brought it to rest in her lap. "North Carolina. My brother came with Colonel Howe to help Woodford."

"You are not married then?"

"Not yet. But there was naught back home. Our parents was gone a long time ago. So me and Elias went to the army together."

"I'm surprised to find so many women in the camp," Clementine said.

"There's not that many, Mrs. Foster." Mary looked at Jane. "There is only ten of us here."

"Are you safe?"

"Oh, yes, ma'am. Those men are too tired for much more than eating what we cook 'em. And they're plenty glad for clean clothes—"

"And mending. They tear up more articles than I thought possible."

They laughed together as only the companions of hardship could. They were in the army together, like the soldiers, they would never be the same.

Amity yearned for such companionship of her own. She did not share this type of closeness with any other creature.

"Although, our Jane here has a beau."

Red blazed up Jane's face. "He is not my beau. He is a respectable gentleman from Norfolk."

"Well, be that as it may. You haven't seen the last of Mr. Clement. Of that I am sure."

12

If he didn't know better, he would think the stone in his hand exerted a presence. The pattern of sliding its smoothness between his thumb and forefinger and into his palm soothed. Simon rapped on the brown door of John's house.

A servant led him to a green parlor overlooking the street.

Children's voices drifted like random notes escaping a ball room.

"Mr. Parchment says he will be with you directly," the servant said before quickly exiting the room again.

"Mr. Morgan," Mrs. Blackstone smirked her way past the servant into the room. "How good of you to call on my last day."

Simon squelched a cringe. "Oh? I hadn't heard you were leaving."

"Unfortunately, I must. Urgent business calls me back to Fredericksburg." She cast her eyes down in what he supposed was an attempt at a demure look, and moved a couple of steps closer. "What do you have there?"

Before he could react, his stone was in her hands. She turned from him to hold the stone up to the window light. "A gift?" The usual clear green appeared cloudy.

"No—"

"It is the most beautiful stone I've ever seen." She swung around toward him.

He held his palm out. "Give it back."

Her smile broadened. A playful glint lit her eyes. "Why is it so important to you?" She sauntered back to the window holding the stone up as she went.

"It doesn't concern you."

"What doesn't concern whom?"

Mrs. Blackstone spun at Parchment's inquiry.

Simon kept his eye on the stone. "Mrs. Blackstone took my stone and refuses to return it."

She rolled her eyes and handed it to Simon. "'Twas taken in jest, Mr. Parchment, as I am sure your Mr. Morgan understood."

A cold rock landed in his palm. He didn't hear her parting words because his stone was once again clear. Of that he was certain, unlike the possible glowing he might have seen by the tree.

John waited for her to leave before drawing close to Simon.

"Are you mad? You can't show that stone to anyone."

"Calm down, John."

John paced.

Simon slid the stone back into his pocket. "I am glad you came when you did."

"I didn't realize you were interested in Winifred."

"I'd just as soon dance with a walking rattlesnake."

"Then why flirt?"

"I wasn't. And if she was, it was poorly done. She's much too old to play the part of a simpering schoolgirl."

"Why did you come?"

"To tell you I'm leaving in the morning. I promised Reed that I would escort his daughter and her aunt to Winchester. I will look in on you after I return if you like."

"There hasn't been sufficient time to receive an answer to our letters."

"There is no real hurry is there? The stone will be safe with me, and if I never know what it is it will be no great loss, will it?"

John stood motionless. "I suppose not, but if it is what we think it is people will be after it. It could make you very rich man."

"I am not in need of funds. And that assumes that I would be willing to part with it, which I am not. So it's moot. And I'm off to Winchester."

"Perhaps we could meet in Fredericksburg."

"I hardly think you need to go to that much trouble."

"The men we're talking about will not consider it any trouble, besides, a couple of them live in Fredericksburg."

"I leave tomorrow."

"Perhaps I'll see you there."

"Suit yourself. But I will not wait for you."

~*~

"Packing is easier this time since we already packed what we needed for this trip." Lucy said as she laid Amity's red print cotton dress in the trunk. "I never will understand why you think you need to go running to and fro over this earth."

"Truth is I'd like to stay here a few more days, but Aunt Clementine will not budge. We are leaving tomorrow."

"Ever since we was children you been runnin'. To and fro, to and fro…"

Amity jumped onto the bed with a huff. "I want to travel. To see things and learn their stories." She stood back up. "My father tells me I can't because I'm a woman—a girl—in his eyes I'm not even a woman at twenty-five."

"Parents always think of their babies as babies."

"Don't you wish you were free to travel around like a man? Visit what you wish, talk to whom you wish?"

Lucy quickly shut the door.

Amity reached for Lucy's hand. "I'm so sorry. I forget sometimes. I think of you as my friend."

"From you, Miss Amity, I accept. Because you is my friend, as much as you can be." A glow infused Lucy's face. "Do I wish to be free? Oh, yes."

Amity wished with all her soul that she could tell Lucy of her father's plans to release his slaves. She'd given her word and could not break it. The consequences were grave if anyone knew of his plans before he could implement them. She stopped cold. Shame ran its course through her midsection and squeezed. Lucy was hers. Her father had given Lucy to her for her eighteenth birthday.

"Your father is a good man, Miss Amity. He don't break up families or nothin', but freedom…" With a faraway look, Lucy picked up another dress.

Amity collected her ink and quills to place in her traveling desk. There had to be a way. Field's wife had freed two of her slaves. "Lucy, how much money do you have?"

Lucy snapped back to the present. "Not much Miss Amity, I'll get it for you if you need it." She turned toward the door then spun back around. "Whatch you need it for?"

"Freedom. Go get it."

"I don't leave that nowhere 'cept right here." Lucy raised her petticoat to reveal a large pocket. She pulled out a small handful of coins that amounted to ten dollars.

"Where did you get so much money?"

"I got nothing to spend it on much, so I saves it. Maybe one day I'll have enough to buy my freedom."

"Put it back and keep it safe." Amity tugged at her bottom lip. She would need to talk to her father. Lucy's ten dollars wasn't enough, but Amity wasn't interested in the money. Lucy needed a stake. Amity could not set her free and expect her to survive with no money. Amity beckoned Lucy to sit on the bed. "I'm not exactly sure how to go about doing this, but we'll try." Amity explained the rudiments of the plan. "First, we will see a lawyer. I don't want you to ever have to watch your back."

"Miss Amity." Lucy's eyes filled with mist. "Are you sure about this?"

Amity took Lucy's work-worn hand in hers. "I am only ashamed I didn't think of it before. I go on and on about being free." She hung her head. "One thing I do know is that after you are free you have to leave Virginia." Amity glanced at her trunk, open with dresses laid neatly inside. Dresses lay on every chair and the bed. "The clothes you need will be easy enough; you've been wearing my clothes for years."

Lucy blushed. "You didn't mind."

"Didn't even think about it. Now you need stylish things. The kind of things a free young lady wears. We can start with this one."

Amity slid the red printed cotton from her trunk and held it up to Lucy's shoulders. "You're a little fuller than me in some places but we can let this one out. At least we're the same height. Will you mind leaving Virginia?"

Lucy's eyes so wide her eyebrows nearly collided with her hairline. "Will I mind going to a country where I can be free? Where my children will be free? No. I don't mind leaving Virginia."

Amity gave her two more dresses to let out during the trip. The next big town would be Fredericksburg. Their secret should be safe until then. Meanwhile she would have to figure out how to get Lucy a large enough stake and let her father know her plans.

Before dawn the next morning, Amity stood before her father in her uncle's book room.

"You remember your promise?" her father asked.

How could she forget she promised to marry the one man in the entire world that wouldn't suit? One who was clearly interested in another woman. "There is nothing to worry about. Aunt Clementine will be with me the entire time."

"Don't dissemble."

"Yes. I remember my promise."

He raised one eyebrow.

"I promise I will marry Simon Morgan, *if*, and it is a very large if, I am compromised on this trip." *And there is no other way out.*

The corners of his mouth lifted as he stepped forward to gently place his hands on her shoulders. She gazed into his gray eyes.

"When did you get to be so grown up?"

Amity placed her head on his shoulder. "I love you, Papa."

"I love you too, Muffin."

She nestled further into his arms and squeezed. She didn't remember the last time he'd called her that. "Are you worried?"

"Of course I am. I'm always worried about you and your brothers and sisters."

"But—"

"But I trust the Almighty to keep you while you travel."

"If I don't try, Papa, I'll never know."

"And if you don't know you'll never rest."

She stepped out of his embrace to see his face. "You understand?"

"Maybe just a little."

"May I ask you a question?"

He inclined a little closer.

"You gave Lucy to me when I turned eighteen."

He closed his eyes in agreement.

"So she belongs to me do with as I choose."

He folded his arms. "Within limits. I would not allow you to abuse her in any way."

"Of course not, but if I wanted to—" She scuffed her foot on the floor "—say, sell her. It would be my choice."

"Is something wrong with Lucy that you want to sell her?"

"No, nothing like that. I just wondered. It will be a long trip and all kinds of things can happen on a long trip."

A light sparked in his eyes. Had he figured it out? "Of course she is yours to do with as you please. I always have my lawyer draw up those kinds of papers. It doesn't hurt if he witnesses the transaction either. That way all can be proved as done properly."

Clementine's voice echoed through the entire house. "Amity!"

Amity swung around at the call.

"Just one more thing, my dear. Remember that Lucy's family is still at the Hall."

Guilt. Would she never be free from its grasp? "I will remember."

She hugged him once more, just in case they ran out of time before leaving.

Her aunt marched through the door. "There you are. Listen." She crooked a finger at Amity and spun to leave again. Amity followed her aunt into the kitchen. "Did you pack extra blankets for Mr. Morgan? It will be a cold ride, and we don't want him freezing to death."

"Yes, Aunt." Not only had she packed blankets for Simon, but also an extra one for Clementine. Amity had even asked Cook to place an extra brick in the oven for her aunt. She'd seemed less hearty the last few days. The last thing she wanted was for her aunt to fall ill just because Amity wanted to see the mountains.

When Amity asked if Clementine would like to put off the trip, she had been vigorous in her denial. "I will go to see my friends in Winchester whether you chose to accompany me or not. You seem to forget that it was my travel the two of you interrupted with your arrival a couple of weeks ago. I have every intention of getting out of this city." Now here they were, on the verge of leaving.

They both said their goodbyes to Amity's Papa before stepping into the coach.

"Will you stop fidgeting? You're making me nervous."

"Sorry, Aunt. I feel like I've forgotten something, and I cannot for the life of me remember what it is."

"Pen?"

Amity nodded.

"Paper?"

"And ink, yes, I have those things."

"Then you have the essentials. Anything you've really forgotten we can pick up along the way."

"Perhaps it is the last minute feel—I mean I have

always wanted to see the mountains, now I'm going, and I wish I was staying."

Clementine laughed. "Isn't that always the way?" she asked, pulling her knitting out of a basket into her lap. Coming off her needles were a fine pair of indigo stockings.

Amity sat back next to her aunt and ran through her list again. What a ninny, for the last five years at least she'd wished to be heading toward the mountains. Where was the joy she should be feeling? Maybe it was Simon unsettling her nerves. She hadn't seen him since the night he brought her home from the ball. He didn't like her stepping into the unruly crowd that was clear enough. What would he think of her plan for Lucy?

The coach pulled to a stop in front of Anderson's. Simon stepped out into the street. After seeing to his trunk, he opened the door and sat opposite Amity. He laid his rifle across the seat behind him and placed a valise appearing to be full of books on the seat. "Good morning, Mrs. Foster, Amity."

"Did I mistake seeing *two* horses attached to our trunk wagon?"

Simon rubbed his hands as if to warm them. "You did not mistake, Mrs. Foster." His words were for her aunt, but he looked only at her. "It's a fine day now that the wind has died down so I took the liberty of assuming...I thought Amity might like to ride?"

Feet flat on the floorboards, she slid to the edge of her seat. "I'd love to ride."

Clementine chuckled, "Well, get on with it then.

You're holding all of us up."

With a grin at Simon, Amity lighted from the coach. Next to Simon's stallion, Pilgrim, stood a sorrel pacer.

"This is Ruby. The finest of Mr. Anderson's somewhat picked-over livery."

Amity approached, Ruby nodded her head and nuzzled Amity's offered hand.

Amity's breath hitched when Simon opened his arms to help her mount. She released him as soon as she attained her saddle hoping he didn't hear the thudding of her rebellious heart.

The coaches pulled away.

"It is a fine day. Thank you for thinking of a ride for me."

"You are welcome. I thought you might enjoy getting out of the coach for a while. No doubt there will be plenty of days we will be glad of its shelter."

They made their way to the front of the little wagon train.

"How are your sister's horses doing?"

"Very well, from what I understand. She had her eye on a new stallion not far from my aunt and uncle's in Kemp's Landing. The unrest there has hampered her efforts."

"She is still in Kemp's Landing?"

"Yes. She'd be safer at home, but I cannot persuade her to return."

"And yet, you travel to Williamsburg during this uncertain time for your own intellectual pursuits."

He grinned again. "Fair point."

"Women have not been excluded from God's gifts, Simon."

He reined Pilgrim to a stop. "Whatever made you say such a thing?"

Amity guided Ruby past him.

He continued. "My sister is free to pursue her goals with horses or whatever business she chooses. But I remain responsible for her safety."

Amity still said nothing.

"Like it or not, women are not the same as men."

"We are different. Not less."

Had she overheard his conversation with her father? Simon remained silent, thinking she would continue.

"Did you tell my father?"

"I didn't have to."

"That explains it."

Simon's mind whirled. "Explains what?"

"Why my father practically shoved us out the door."

"Surely you can understand his point."

"I understand that he thinks he's caring for me. What he doesn't understand is that I am a grown woman."

"On the contrary—"

Lucy peered wide eyed out of the traveling coach. They'd reached the bend in the road to Sweet Hall Ferry. It was time to cross the river. She should have prepared Lucy more for these crossings.

"Excuse me." Amity lined her position with the traveling coach and gave Lucy a reassuring nod.

Lucy's head retreated.

"Is there something wrong?"

"Lucy is afraid of water."

"She will be all right. Jax and the other servants will be with her."

"I will cross with her."

"Amity, I can't leave you to cross alone with the servants, and I hardly think your aunt would like to join you."

The lane narrowed as they reached the other side of the bend. Amity and Simon trotted to the front of the line.

A breeze chilled Amity's neck and challenged her hat to remain in place.

The Pamunkey River lined the horizon.

"I shall be fine with Lucy."

13

Five servants, two coaches, eight horses, two women, and him. The ferry could hold one coach at a time with one or two people, not including the ferryman. Simon divided and re-divided the problem. Why did the woman have to be so difficult?

He ran his free hand over his thigh. His thumb brushed the stone resting in his pocket. At his side was the woman he'd dreamed about for the past ten years. If he had to ride the ferry six times himself, he would see to it that her wish was met.

High on a bluff across the Pamunkey sat the Claiborne home. He'd heard that Claiborne removed west and a Mr. Ruffin lived there now and ran the ferry.

"Stop worrying, Simon." Amity nudged beside him as the coach rolled onto the ferry behind nickering horses. "I know you promised my father to look out for me. You will be able to see me from Claiborne's. I've known these servants all my life. None of them will harm me."

"This will be an issue at each crossing, won't it?"

The sun glinted off Amity's red-brown curls as she nodded. "Yes."

Stomach tightening, Simon took his place next to

Izzy James

her aunt on the flat-bottomed boat. He watched Amity get smaller with each stride across the river and thanked God for Jax.

Clementine slid her hand on Simon's arm. "She's stubborn like her father."

Simon glanced at the woman on his arm. Her gaze was directed across the river as well.

"She is also as generous as her mother, and tender-hearted."

Simon swallowed the only comment he could think of which questioned the rightness of her mind.

"Tenderness she gets from both of them."

"Are you saying she will temper with time?"

"Not at all. I expect she'll get more daring."

~*~

"Whatchoo afraid of, Miss Lucy?" Jax leaned against the coach wheel.

"I don't like the river." Lucy kept her eyes on the water lapping at the sandy ramp. Amity stood at her friend's side,

Amity could still taste the water as it went up her nose as she fought the overseer her father had hired. She and Lucy had been thirteen. Amity had gone down to the river that miserable, hot summer day to cool her feet. She arrived at the river edge just in time to see the man with Lucy waist-deep in water. Lucy's soaked dress clung to her young body. The man had Lucy by the arms, leaning over her, causing an unnatural arc that forced her head closer to submersion.

Anger surged past the quaking in her stomach. Amity plunged into the water to Lucy's side at once. "Let her go right this minute, Mr. Clapper."

The startled man peered over his shoulder. "Get outta here, Miss Amity. This doesn't concern you."

"You'll do as I say." Amity used the sternest voice she could muster hoping they couldn't hear the quaking in her stomach. She grabbed his arm, trying to get him away from Lucy.

He shook her off. "I see I'll have to have a talk with your father about your behavior toward your elders." Clapper sneered.

Fear leapt in Amity's heart as he pushed Lucy down again. Lucy's arms windmilled and then went limp. Amity reached out to grab Lucy's arm.

"Let her go!"

Clapper elbowed Amity away.

"Clapper, stop. You'll do as I say." Field's voice carried over the water.

Amity's thumping heart filled with relief.

Clapper grimaced and shoved Lucy further under the salty water.

Lucy's hands flapped, and she sputtered to the surface, fighting Clapper, and heaving as she tried to breathe.

Field walked toward them, never hesitating as he entered the water.

Amity pushed Mr. Clapper and he toppled. She grabbed her friend by the hand and led her away as Clapper fumbled and splashed for his footing. She and Lucy came out of the river. Amity took off running to the house, dragging a wet and breathless Lucy behind her. She'd left Field to deal with Mr. Clapper. At dinner that evening, she heard that Mr. Clapper had moved on.

Jax's soothing voice drew Amity away from the horrible memory.

"Nothin' goin' to happen to you on the river this day, Miss Lucy. See it's calm today. If we wasn't travelin' I'd see about doing me a spot of fishin.'"

"If'n you got permission from Mr. Simon: you mean. You ain't free to do a spot a fishin'"

Jax stood a little taller and puffed out his chest. "Now that's where I got you, Miss Lucy. I'm free. Mr. Simon's father left me free in his will when he died."

Lucy blushed. "I'm sorry, Mr. Jax, I…" She shuffled. "I mean it's wonderful—I'm sorry I thought otherwise."

"Nothing for you to be sorry about, Miss Lucy. It's an easy enough conclusion to reach."

"If you're free, why do you stay here?"

"Well, now, that's a different question. Sometimes I think I'm gonna pick up and head out there to see what I can find." He drew a broad sweep with his hand. "Then I think, it's gonna be more grass and sky and trees and I got that where I'm at." He looked down into her eyes. "I guess I just haven't found reason enough to leave yet."

A hint of color flushed Lucy's cheeks.

"You stick close to me, nothin' goin' to happen to you on the river this day."

"He's right." Mr. Ruffin rocked the raft as he

hopped aboard. He cast away from the shore. "With the winds we had the last few days I couldn't think of running the ferry. Blew shingles right off the house. But today's all right."

The conversation turned to shingles and rooftop repairs.

As the ferry slowly made its way across Pamunkey, Lucy stood close to Jax.

Amity gazed around. Across the river Simon watched their progress. Really, what exactly did he think was likely to happen right here in full view of everybody? She held her tongue until the last of their retinue crossed the river and she and Simon had remounted. "I'm a grown woman, Simon."

"You have said that to me before."

"To no effect, apparently."

"I promised your father."

"What? What did you promise him, to stifle my experience? To be distrustful of my decisions?"

"To protect you. And your aunt. Neither of you seem to understand the danger a trip such as this poses."

"Not as much as—" She urged Ruby forward lest she say something she would regret. Not at Simon, but about her own life. She loved her parents. She loved her siblings. What drove her to be adventurous she couldn't say.

Mill's Ordinary appeared. The flat-faced building was covered in white clapboard, had black-shuttered windows, and looked as if it would tumble into the road if tapped just the right way. A tall, boney man met them in the yard. "Mrs. Foster's party?"

"Yes." Simon answered stepping in front of Amity. She gave her reins to the boy that arrived soon after his master and went to greet her aunt.

"It is a blessing to stand on solid ground, is it not?" Clementine smoothed her hair. "A good walk is what I'd like to have as soon as we've dined."

"Mr. Grimes." The tavern keeper introduced himself to Simon and turned. "Mrs. Foster, may I say it is a pleasure to see you once again?"

"Thank you, Mr. Grimes."

"May I also say that Mrs. Grimes and I were sorry to hear about Mr. Foster."

Clementine's eyes moistened. "Thank you again, Mr. Grimes." She retrieved a handkerchief from her basket. "I wish to dine as soon as is practicable. We are famished."

"We are prepared. Perhaps you would care to freshen yourselves while Mrs. Grimes lays the table?"

"That is satisfactory."

Amity followed Clementine into the house, Simon at her back.

A small fire smoldered in the fireplace in the bright bedroom. In the center was a large wooden, canopied bed she would share with her aunt. Three smaller beds lined the walls for their servants.

"Your uncle and I stayed here often when we traveled this way."

A tug of grief pulled at Amity's heart. Clementine and Uncle William were the only people whose marriage mirrored her own parents'. More than best friends, her mother called it, so much more. She had hoped for the same in her own marriage, back when she thought she would marry Simon and have twenty children. Those were long ago days and she wouldn't let that ruin her adventure. "It must be hard…"

"It is hard, child, but such is life. I'm not the first person to lose their husband and I won't be the last. I trust that God will take care of me."

"Me, too, but it does make me wonder if it's worth it."

"I wouldn't trade the life I had with William because of the grief I feel now. I will see him again, and to that I cling. God is not done with me yet." Clementine wiped the mist from her eyes and took Amity's hand. "And He's just beginning with you. You've been given great opportunity so don't waste it."

"You mean this trip?"

"Precisely. There are decisions to be made on this trip that will impact your entire existence."

"I know what you mean. I have been overwhelmed at what types of books I should be writing. I have written only stories for my siblings. When I planned this trip, I assumed I would write about Virginia at War. Now I'm thinking only of how to explain what I've seen to my sisters and brothers."

"That is not precisely what I meant. Amity, if you want a man to treat you like a grown woman you have to respect his need to be a man."

"What does that mean?"

Clementine patted her hand. "Shall we check on

Mrs. Grimes? I declare my leather bag is looking a might tasty at the moment and that can't be any good."

A conspicuous silence filled the main chamber. It had to be the first day she'd seen no soldiers. Certainly, there were none in the dining chamber now. Simon stood by a window. A young couple engaged in lively conversation occupied one of the other tables in the room. Platters of roasted fowls and winter vegetables waited at the largest table in the room. Simon held her aunt's chair, Clementine winked. Amity waited for Simon to hold her chair.

"How was your ride, Mr. Morgan?" Clementine asked.

"Enjoyable, but I am glad to have my feet on the ground for a while."

Amity nodded her agreement. Ruby's gait eased her way immeasurably, but it did not make up for Amity's lack of practice. She was tired. All she wanted was time with pen and paper. So many impressions to record. The comment from her aunt still rankled. What exactly did Aunt Clementine mean when she said men needed room to be men? Seemed to Amity that men had all the room they needed to do whatever it was they wanted to do.

The room filled one by one as their dinner progressed. Light from the fine day outside softened into twilight.

"I believe I shall have to forgo my idea of walking before bed." Clementine yawned deeply. "It will be another long day tomorrow, so I shall say good night."

Amity followed her aunt. None of her rosy

thoughts of scribbling her daily impressions each night had accounted for the lack of privacy that would be necessary for this trip. She could hardly sit with her candle while her aunt tried to sleep. She gathered her notebook, pen, and ink, and went back downstairs.

A few men remained in the main chamber talking amongst themselves.

Mr. Grimes met her at the entrance and directed her to a more secluded room across from the main dining chamber.

"Amity." Simon waved her over to a table by the fire. "It's hardly a quiet place to work."

"Aunt Clementine is asleep already and there is nowhere else to be."

"Sometimes I do my best thinking in coffee shops."

"That's hard to believe. How do you think?"

"Something about the world going on around me. As though it's taking care of itself and can do without me for a little while." He glanced down at the table with a hint of rose in his cheeks.

A door clicked open in her heart. "I'm afraid I'd find it too distracting to go to bed when a party is going on downstairs."

Simon drew up and leaned back in his chair, loose limbs draping over chair arms, legs spread out. "Your father told me you are working on a book."

It was Amity's cheeks on fire now. "At first I thought I wanted to travel to write better books for my sisters and brothers. Then I got to Williamsburg, and I met those women, and I knew I needed to tell their stories. Now we are on our way to Winchester and I feel I should write about my travels. You might well say I'm in a quandary."

Simon sipped his coffee.

"It's all right if you laugh now."

"I'll not laugh."

"Oh, scolding then. List for me the reasons why I shouldn't pursue writing." She counted them on her fingers; "The doors are closed to women…it's too dangerous for a woman to travel."

"I'm not doing that either."

"Why not?"

"I don't know, maybe because it's not the kind of thing you say to your friends."

Wonderment blew through her mind like a freshening wind. "Do you think we can be friends?"

"I think so, don't you?"

"I've never had a male friend before. They were always suitors or Field's friends—like you."

"With only one sister I never really had the choice."

Amity must have looked puzzled for he continued, "We only had each other, so we became close. I like to think Hester and I are friends."

The faces of her siblings played across her memory. "There's so many of us—I am not sure we are friends—it feels like we never quite have enough time. There's always something to be done for one of us. I guess I'm closer to Field than the others, but I love them all."

"I always envied Field that problem. My ideal is to

have a house filled with little voices."

"It is not all joyful sounds."

"I'm sure not, but it must be better than the silence of my house."

Drunken voices leaked into the room.

"Would you care to walk? I expect the evening will be as fine as the day."

On the porch, Amity drew her woolen shawl closer wrapping her hands underneath to keep them warm.

"It's crisper than I thought it would be." Simon rubbed his hands together for warmth. "Would you care to go back inside?"

"Not at all. It was getting stuffy in there with the fires and all those men."

Simon crooked his arm. Amity placed her hand on his sleeve, and the gnats returned to her belly. Stepping through golden rectangles of light they made their way to the back of the tavern. Beyond the kitchen and other dependencies lay a dirt track through a harvested field. Moonlight dimmed the stars.

"Why did you agree to accompany us?"

"Look, just because you ask a question does that mean I have to answer it?"

"I thought you said we were friends. My friends and I talk about everything. Certainly, something as simple as why we went on a trip."

Animals snuffled in stable as they traversed its length.

"Everything?"

Amity was quiet for moment while she thought.

"Yes. I can't think of anything I would need to keep from Robertine Glassock. Only mundane things that would bore her curls straight."

Simon rasberried, took a deep breath, and snorted. An outright laugh shook her hand from his arm.

Amity stared at him. By now, he was bent with laughter. If he stood up, she expected tears. "What is so funny?"

He gasped for air.

Amity released an embarrassed giggle.

"An image of my sister, Hester." He gasped. "Curls straight out...one at a time as she listened to me talk..." He curled over again. Strangled laughter escaped.

Amity gave him an indulgent grin. Then in her mind's eye an image appeared of Aunt Clementine at the dinner table with Papa. Papa loved to talk politics. Ping! One of Aunt Clementine's curls pulled out straight. Papa continued. Ping! Another. Clementine was unaware that her lack of interest was showing as one by one her curls straightened and stuck straight up...soon Amity's laughter blended with Simon's. Amity grabbed his arm to keep from landing on the damp ground. He placed his hand over hers. Tears still streaming, she finally stopped laughing.

Simon quieted.

Amity stopped breathing.

Simon leaned toward her as he straightened.

A breath passed between them.

"Park 'em over there!" The stable hand shouted to the rider.

The intimacy between them evaporated in the voices from the barn.

"Well, this is awkward." Amity looked at the ground and then to the sky.

"It is." Simon took her hand and placed it back on his arm. "I'll take you back in."

Every limb was alive. She wanted to jump and run. "It is a fine night though."

"Yes, but your aunt was right. It will be a long day tomorrow, and we should get some rest."

14

"You will miss riding today, I think." Clementine didn't look up from her stitches as the coach pulled away from the ordinary.

Mr. Grimes had no replacement for Ruby, who trotted back to Williamsburg behind the rider who came to fetch her last night. Amity found she didn't mind a little time and space to put Simon Morgan back in the place she'd kept him in her mind for the past ten years.

"It is another glorious day," Amity sat her travel desk on her lap. "But I shall try to put the time to good use." She anchored a clean sheet of paper with one thumb turning her gaze out the window to order her thoughts.

Simon touched his hat in greeting.

Her belly got the jitters. She inclined her head. He made her feel like a grown woman and a schoolgirl all at once. Last night they laughed like she hadn't laughed since they were pranking children. Last night. He would have kissed her if the rider had not arrived when he did. She was sure of it. Her first real kiss. Old dreams revived at the thought. He might try tonight if Clementine was absent again after dinner. "How are you feeling today, Aunt?"

She really must get these feelings in check. She decided her future with him years ago. She wasn't about to change her mind on a bit of whimsy. Friends is what they decided. Just friends. It was for the best.

"I am very well. I pray our accommodations at Emerson's this evening will be as clean as Mill's was last night."

"I am truly glad."

"Me, too. I'm not one to lay about, but a good night's sleep is not to be underestimated."

Simon's movement outside her window caught her eye once again.

Simon nodded ahead and sped out in front of them. He sat his horse as though Pilgrim was an extension of his own long limbs.

The coach dipped into a close wood. Shadow filled the conveyance with damp March cold. The last hint of warmth was gone from her brick. She placed the extra blanket over Clementine's knees.

The ground beneath them got rougher as though they traveled across a road woven of tree limbs. Amity lurched from side to side. She gave up on anchoring the page and tossed it into her desk.

Aunt Clementine dropped her needles and braced herself against the coach walls.

The coach slowed.

"At this pace we won't see Emerson's tonight."

"It's bound to get better soon, Aunt."

"William traveled up and down these parts. He knew all the good places to stay. I don't remember him saying anything about a place between here and

Tappahannock. Of course if it was rough he rode his horse and did not tumble around in a carriage." Sadness deepened the gray in her hazel eyes.

"We'll make it. Simon will make sure we get through."

"What makes you so sure?"

"He's like Field."

"Is he?" A mischievous smile hung about her lips.

"It is a reasonable thing to recognize someone's good qualities without needing to marry them."

"Hmmph."

The crack of the wheel reverberated through the woods. The coach listed to its right side and stopped.

Amity gave Clementine a steadying hand. When she pushed, the door bounced off a tree on the side of the narrow lane.

Simon waited on the other side to help them down.

"Damage?" Clementine didn't wait to head to the broken wheel on the other side.

"The wheel gonna have to come off," Jax hollered.

Simon's hands on her waist once again sent the gnats swirling. Her gaze caught his. Anxiety spiked in their depths. "I'm safe."

Relief caressed his features.

Did he feel it too?

Thick forest began barely two feet from the broken wheel. A frisson of energy infused Amity when she brushed against Simon as they squeezed shoulder to shoulder to get a better look.

"Reparable here, I think. It will take a little time. If

we packed..." Simon said.

"We got tools and some wood back in the luggage wagon, Mr. Simon. But that wheel gonna have to come off."

"How far back?"

"Not too far, be here just in time for us to break out something to eat."

"The food is in that wagon."

Jax grinned. "Yes, Miss Amity, but if we was to have food and take it out, and make us ready to eat, right as we set down, the other wagon will be here."

"Yes, well. What do we do in the meantime?" Clementine drew her cloak around her. "I'm freezing."

The coach door swung open when Simon touched the latch. "Seems steady enough." He pushed against the sides before he pulled out a traveling blanket for Clementine. To Jax he said, "We scout out something to prop it up with while we get the wheel off and repair it."

Amity stepped up behind him. "Let me get my things off."

"There's not that much."

She grinned at him. "Surely you don't need to be lifting traveling bricks for no reason."

He bowed away with a flourish. "We shall procure a wedge." He and Jax stepped into the woods.

Shortly after she'd stacked the traveling bricks and the small bags next to a tree root well out of the way, the rustle of their second wagon echoed in the woods.

Jax and George took a saw to a fallen tree a few feet from the road.

Lucy prepared a meal of bread and ham. It was gone before Amity saw any crumbs to clean up the three men stood to appraise the damage once again.

Jax rolled the log next to the coach.

Jax and George stood on either side of the wheel. Jax stood head to head with Simon. George wasn't much taller than Amity's five feet.

"If I push it up, you could stand up the log," Jax said.

Pointing to the coach, Lucy interrupted. "Jax, you can't push that thing all by yourself. Let George help, I can stand that log under there."

Simon removed his coats leaving him in his shirt sleeves.

Amity shifted her gaze to the much safer Lucy to keep from staring at Simon.

"Jax and I will lift. George, you stand the log," Simon ordered.

Lucy's mouth firmed into a straight line. Obviously, she didn't think that would work either.

Amity agreed and took her place beside Lucy ready to dive under and push the supporting log into place.

Jax stood at the rear side of the wheel with Simon at the front side. The two men placed their backs to the coach and bent their knees.

"You ready?" Simon called to George.

George squatted behind the log. "Yes."

On the count of three, Simon lifted. The coach raised a breath from the ground.

George thudded the stump against the bottom of

the coach.

They let the coach down slowly. George stayed in position.

Simon peered at Jax. "One more time."

Jax nodded.

Simon took a breath that expanded his chest. Amity thought his fitted shirt might rip from the pressure of his strength. They lifted, and George fitted the log in place.

Simon clapped Jax on the back. The two men stood. Simon flexed, stretching arms over his head.

Amity couldn't look away from Simon's muscles this time.

~*~

The horizon had softened into a red-orange haze, and a stiff wind joined them by the time they reached Tappahannock. Soreness reminded Simon of the muscles he needed to exercise more often. Traveling always interfered with his regimen. But this journey was worth every inconvenience he'd encountered so far.

Mrs. Foster's husband had indeed known what he was about in choosing accommodations. Mill's had been clean and the food respectable. Tonight they were to lodge at Emerson's. If reports were correct, they were in for more of the same. Clean beds and Mrs. Emerson's reputation in the kitchen were renown.

It looked no different from other ordinaries. White clapboard, black shutters, large porch on the front, and five dormers across the roof. Friendly light shown from clean window lights. Mrs. Emerson ordered the care of their horses and carriages. Once she directed her staff, she led them into a private dining chamber.

"Well, let's hope that will be our only adversity on this trip." Clementine said as she relaxed into a chair.

"We have a long way to go Mrs. Foster."

"I understand that, Mr. Morgan."

They took the rest of the meal in silence. Simon found Mrs. Emerson's bread earned its reputation, crusty on the outside and soft on the inside. He inhaled the first piece before the fresh churned butter melted. He hadn't realized how hungry he'd gotten in the cold. He could have ridden in the carriage with Amity and her aunt, but he'd rather face the cold than the awkwardness in the carriage. He took a deep drink of warm coffee. The liquid slid down into his middle, and held in place by the bread, warmed him.

Laughing with Amity last night took Simon back to their young courtship. He didn't kiss her then because Field was his best friend. She'd been so young. Too young to know what she wanted, at least, that's what he thought at the time. He'd miscalculated about her knowing her own mind then; he wasn't about to make that mistake again.

The way Amity'd lingered in his arms when he lowered her out of the broken carriage suggested the awkwardness was behind them, but he never knew with Amity. He'd yet to decipher the mystery of her stormy eyes.

"Would you care for a walk tonight, Simon?"

"I thought after today you would both prefer to sit by the fire and stay warm."

"Exactly what I intend to do, Mr. Morgan," Clementine said. "I plan to spend the evening with Mrs. Peabody on her latest adventure, tucked next to the fire in my room."

Amity's rose lips smoothed into a grin. "I thought to take a look around Tappahannock. It's my first time here. Unless you think the day is too far gone." Her challenge was unmistakable.

"No, in fact I see the gamers are starting to arrive in our hosts' main chamber." Clementine nodded her disapproval toward the room behind Simon.

"I'd be happy to escort you around the neighborhood if that is what you would like…"

"I would." Amity followed her aunt upstairs and returned wearing her heavy woolen cloak. A soft charge sparked under his skin when she lightly placed her hand on his offered arm.

Cold, hard dirt packed streets tamped the sounds of boots and wheels as people moved around the village. From Water Lane they took a right on to Prince Street. On their immediate left The Scots Arms Tavern hummed with sounds of tinkling glass and laughter. In the next block on the right side of the street candles glowed in the windows of Whitlock's Ordinary, where more men sat around tables shuffling cards. Shouts and laughter spilled into the street.

"Shall we turn around? It seems that all Tappahannock is gaming tonight."

Amity said nothing but deftly followed his lead

when he headed them past the taverns once more. "'Tis a busy place."

Simon only nodded. It was his job on this trip to keep Amity out of danger while she explored the world she had yet to see. Hopefully, there was more to see of this town than rowdy taverns.

The wind had blown off the clouds leaving behind a clock-stopping cold. If he guessed right, the next day would be downright frigid. He should plan on riding in the carriage tomorrow.

In the block past Emerson's a large brick house overlooked the street. Candles in those windows shone on a family in their parlor. A man sat in a high-backed chair with a book by the fire. On the other side, a woman sat with her needlework. Three children were sometimes visible as they moved about.

Amity pulled them to a stop. "Do you suppose that is his wife?"

"Maybe it's his sister that keeps house for him."

"She does favor him a little."

"They say that a man and his wife grow to look like each other as they age."

"They're not aged. They aren't much older than we are."

"But as you say, she does favor him a little. Perhaps we tend to choose people who look like ourselves naturally, without thinking about it at all." Simon mused.

"You don't look like me."

They both stopped.

She quickly looked down the street.

Simon took her hand and brought her back around to face him. "Amity."

She turned her face toward him. He could see her question in the weak candlelight of the parlor window.

"I'm sorry I nearly kissed you last night."

"You are?"

"We said we were friends, and I nearly trespassed—I guess I got carried away."

A deep sigh escaped her lips. "It's all right, Simon. It was almost like we were home again."

"The years fell away, and I felt…"

She took a step back. "Let's not talk about it—there is no need to analyze everything to death." Her hand swiped the air in between them wiping away the momentum building to a second attempt to capture those soft red lips. "Shall we continue our walk?"

He offered his arm. Amity took it lightly and still a spark jolted through him. He could not feel it, for the necessary arm was engaged, but he wondered if the stone was glowing in his pocket. It certainly didn't feel any warmer than it had earlier, but he couldn't be sure since his entire self continued to react to her closeness. "Would you say the world is a magical place?"

"I'm sorry, I didn't hear you, I was thinking about that house and the family in the window."

"What about them?"

"I hope she is his wife and that those three or four heads were their children."

"Do you?" A smile came up from somewhere deep inside. Perhaps the Amity he'd known so many years ago wasn't that far gone after all.

15

Amity arrived back in her room to find her aunt asleep by the fire. The volume of *Mrs. Peabody's Adventure in Scotland* sat open on her chest. Too flustered to sleep, and too cold to sit at the small desk provided, Amity retrieved her lap desk from her case and sat on the opposite side of the fire hoping her aunt would waken. Not that she knew what she would say. She couldn't very well be disappointed that the man she flatly refused by reason of unsuitability wouldn't kiss her. That the laughter they'd shared the night before melted the years away and her heart reacted to him as it did when she was fifteen. It was dangerous to think this way. Especially since his heart may truly belong to another.

"His heart doesn't belong to another." Clementine croaked.

"I didn't realize I spoke aloud."

"Simon Morgan has no more interest in Winifred Blackstoke than you do."

"Blackstone."

"What?"

"Her name is Winifred Blackstone."

"It doesn't matter what her name is, he isn't interested." Clementine continued to croak over a parched throat. "Give me some coffee, will you?"

Amity refilled her aunt's dish from the pot on the table between them.

"How do you know that? She is beyond beautiful, and she has a scientific mind. I would never read about electricity unless I absolutely had to, and I pray I never shall."

"Dear child, men do not look to supply themselves with what they already have."

"He told me tonight he was sorry he nearly kissed me—not kissed me—just that he nearly kissed me." Tears threatened. "I can't believe I told you that."

Clementine chuckled. "Child, you do remind me of your father, but the boldness—that comes from your mother."

Amity wiped her eyes.

Her aunt pointed at her. "You may trust me in this. Simon Morgan is biding his time."

"For what?"

"Did you not tell me that you refused him, went so far as to tell him that you thought you wouldn't suit?"

Amity cast her gaze to the fire. "I did."

"That is why he's biding his time. When the time is right, and he is sure of you, then you will hear from him again. Until then, he'll play it safe. Can you blame him?"

"I guess not."

"And listen to me. You must let him move in his own time. Don't do anything. He has to do this for himself or he'll never be sure."

"Sure of what?"

"That he did the right thing. He must believe in himself. And he must know that you believe in him too."

~*~

Thomas stepped into Winfred Blackstone's and closed the door behind him. "I've brought the men, Freddie, but you are making a mistake."

She pointed at him. "Don't you presume to tell me—"

"They are bad men, Freddie."

"Good." Her smile trembled a bit, so she shut her lips. "That's what I need."

"But—"

"Save your breath. I will do what I must to save Wilfred."

"Freddie—"

"Leave."

He turned, placed a hand on the lintel as though he would say more. Took a deep breath. Dropped his hand and left the room. He wouldn't waver, not when it came right down to it. Whatever it was, she'd always been able to count on Thomas Burns. The only man since Charlie who wouldn't cheat her. When this was over, she'd have to think of a way to thank him.

When this was over, she was going to sell the tavern and take Wilfred far away. They'd go wherever he wanted. Somewhere from the picture books he loved. She would spare no expense. And she'd give Thomas enough to make a new life for himself as well.

It was a good plan.

Boot-steps scraped the stairs.

She opened the drawer of her desk to make her loaded pistol easy to grab and steeled herself to meet her enablers. "Thomas!"

He popped his head in the door.

"Send them in."

One tall, the other short. They didn't smell for all they looked like dirt clods. The tall one talked. The short one leered.

Thomas left the door half open.

"Him outside says ye be wanting our services."

The short one revealed a mouthful of blackened teeth and placed one foot closer. "What kind o' service might you be wanting, lady?"

Winifred recoiled.

The tall one put a hand on the chest of his partner.

Thomas stepped into the room.

Winifred straightened. "I should like you to retrieve an item from a gentleman who will arrive here tomorrow evening or possibly the next night."

"And just what might that be?"

Winifred described the stone. "He keeps the stone with him at all times, so you will have to take it from him somewhere. Not here. I do not want any of this to take place here. Do you understand?"

The tall man took affront to her tone. "We understand, lady. We wouldn'ta got where we are today if we didn't understand our business."

The short one showed his teeth again.

"Thomas will send you word when the gentleman

has arrived." She placed a small bag of coins on the table. "The first half. Second half when I have the stone."

The short one retrieved the bag and weighed it in his hand. "Feels about right," And handed it off to the tall one.

The man poured the gold into his palm. "This'll do."

"Thomas will send word."

"We'll be around."

"Not here."

He made a fist around the coin. "I said we understood."

"This way, gentlemen." Thomas waved them toward the door and closed it behind them.

Winifred dropped into her chair to let the trembling dissipate. Then she went to her son's room and climbed into bed.

16

Long journeys make normally embarrassing things less so. The morning meal at Port Royal had been generous, and Amity and Clementine had indulged in an extra dish of coffee. Amity felt not a pang of red face when she required the driver to stop an hour and a half into their journey.

Once again, they travelled on a narrow road lined with dense woods on either side. She and Clementine picked their way through the woods on the right side of the carriage. Simon and the male servants took the left side. A warmer day than the couple they'd spent at Tappahannock, Amity was glad to be out to stretch her legs.

Once safely out of direct site of the carriage Clementine leaned against a tree. Amity went a little off to the left to seek privacy for herself and give her aunt a little as well. Amity righted her skirts and walked back the way she came.

"Amity! Run!" Clementine's screech reached her as she made her way around the large tree that separated them. Clementine stood in front of a large bear. Stiff and moving groggily on all fours, it looked as though it had recently awakened. Behind her Lucy's footsteps cracked twigs.

"Lucy, run!"

Amity ran toward Clementine. There was no way the older woman could outrun a bear. *Dear Lord, don't let it have cubs.*

She reached Clementine as the bear stood on its hind legs. Clementine stuck out her left arm to shield Amity while pushing her with her right hand. The bear swiped. A loud crack burst through the trees. The bear reeled back toppling onto all fours. Another burst and the bear crumpled.

Clementine slipped to the earth. Blood pooled in her lap where she rested her wounded arm.

Simon handed Amity his rifle. He lifted Clementine into his arms and strode quickly through the woods.

"Find brandy and bandages." He called to George, who had been driving the wagon of provisions.

"Stop fussing. I'm all right."

"Place her in the wagon. It's too dark in the carriage." Amity commanded.

Clementine rested against the side boards of the wagon. Amity knelt on the floor. Once in position so she would not touch her aunt needlessly, she gently peeled away the remnants of the cotton print clinging to shredded skin.

"You've got three deep gashes and a fourth that's not as deep. "Amity did not turn to look at Simon standing behind her. "We'd better get going. The sooner we get to a doctor the better."

"Are you sure you are up to it, Mrs. Foster?"

"Yes."

Amity poured water over the gashes.

While they waited for the brandy, Clementine broke out in tremors. Amity covered her with blankets from the carriage. Clementine closed her eyes. Lines of laughter deepened in her pain made the strong face fragile. Amity finger brushed escaped strands from the dear face. After what seemed like three hours, but was probably five minutes, Lucy stood by with strips of clean cloth and a bottle of brandy.

"Are you ready?"

Clementine opened her eyes. Fear sat in the deep recesses of hazel brown gaze, and then firmed into courage. Clementine nodded her head.

Amity nodded back. "I've got you."

"Miss Clementine, I'm coming up there." Clementine's gaze flew to Lucy. She climbed up and over Clementine in a flash, tucked herself in behind the older lady, and nodded. Lucy took her free hand in hers.

Amity uncorked the brandy and got a further nod from Clementine.

Clementine clenched as the brandy hit her wounds and muted a cry. Amity poured one more time for good measure and gingerly wrapped the wounds. Clementine resumed shaking. Simon carried her to the carriage. Amity climbed in first and had Clementine placed in her lap. It was only way she could think to keep her warm and reduce the shaking.

Clementine opened her eyes again. "Mr. Morgan?"

He stopped and looked back at her.

"Thank you."

"You are very welcome. Let's hope this is the last adversity on this trip."

Clementine gave him a shaky grin. "Agreed."

"Simon." Amity hoped her voice was calm.

He turned.

"Perhaps you should ride ahead and make sure a doctor is available when we arrive."

"Not yet," he snapped.

"We'll be all right," She snapped back. "Trust me; no one will get me out of this carriage before we arrive in Fredericksburg."

He rolled his eyes. "We are too far out, Amity. Nothing is to be gained for me to arrive three hours before you do."

Clementine patted her hand. "Let's just go. We are staying at Charlie Blackstone's Tavern."

The bottom went out of Amity's stomach. Blackstone's Tavern? Could it be the same Blackstone? It must be. Mrs. Blackstone came from Fredericksburg, and she'd heard the woman owned a tavern.

"It's the best one in town. My William always stayed there."

Amity squelched her dismay and brushed her fingers over her aunt's forehead. "Don't worry about a thing, Aunt Clementine, rest." Amity faced the window and prayed for health for her aunt and wisdom for herself. A sojourn with Simon and Mrs. Blackstone was the least of her worries. She had plenty to keep her occupied tending her aunt. But she didn't relish the idea one bit.

~*~

Blackstone's did look like the nicest tavern in town. It compared favorably to the large residences they passed as they made their way through the square grid of Fredericksburg. Mr. Burns, a tall man with a sleek figure and black hair tied neatly back in a queue, met their carriage. After hearing about Aunt Clementine's mishap, he sent a boy to get the doctor.

Aunt Clementine opened her eyes as Amity was introduced.

Simon carried Aunt Clementine and followed Mr. Burns to her room.

As they were getting Aunt Clementine settled, the doctor arrived. Quick introductions and a recounting of their adventure took place. The doctor nodded as he listened. After uncorking a bottle, Dr. Solomon gave Clementine a small draft. "This will help with the pain."

In a very few moments, Clementine slackened into the bed. Relief relaxed rigid muscles.

The doctor straightened the arm and removed the bandages. "You have done an admirable job of cleaning the wound, Miss Archer." He worked methodically re-cleaning and stitching each laceration. Dr. Solomon didn't look up until he'd finished. "There is always a risk that she could lose the arm. Your quick action may have saved her that."

"How long will it take before she's better?"

"You should expect to stay here at least a week, maybe ten days."

He left her with a small bottle containing a physic that Clementine could take to sleep. While she still slept, Amity slipped to her own room to retrieve her writing desk. She must write to her father and make him aware of the attack and her aunt's condition. It might be wise for them to turn back once Clementine healed. She couldn't imagine that Clementine would wish to continue after such an ordeal.

The room was as Clementine promised, clean with a warm fire. They were the only guests, so Clementine and Amity had separate rooms. Tonight she would spend next to her aunt, and every night until she knew she was out of danger.

She slipped back into Clementine's room to compose her letters by a small window overlooking the street. A red sunset set her paper aglow before she'd finished her missives.

They were disturbed only by a maid bearing dinner of beef stew and bread. Clementine sipped broth from the stew but wanted nothing heavier.

Amity found her mouth-watering at the aroma and tucked away all her stew and a good slice of bread and butter.

~*~

Simon followed the maid as she went to collect the dinner tray from Clementine's room. Amity was seated by the window.

"How is she?" he asked.

"Mr. Morgan, it would behoove you to practice

whispering, I could hear you all the way over here." Amity's aunt opened her eyes.

"My apologies, Mrs. Foster. I thought I was whispering."

"To answer your question, I'm doing as well as can be expected. Dr. Solomon says I may still lose my arm, but he thinks probably not. We can expect to stay here at least a week."

Concern never left Amity's countenance.

"Now I wish you both to leave me so that I may get some sleep."

"Go ahead Simon. I'll stay with my aunt tonight."

"Leave me, my dear. I'll call if I need you."

"I will stay while you sleep."

"No. I can't sleep with you staring at me. I'm not dying. Go away." She flicked her good hand in dismissal.

Amity gawked.

"I'll see you in the morning. If I need you before then I'll call."

"Promise."

"I promise."

Amity gathered her desk and followed Simon out of the room pulling the door closed.

"What if I can't hear her?"

"Amity!"

She dashed into the room.

"There. You *can* hear me. Now, go away." Clementine winked.

Amity's breath rushed out and with it the anxiety that had kept her rigid all day.

"Would you care to take a walk? Stretch your legs?" Simon asked.

"Yes, she would." Clementine called from her bed. "Lucy!"

Lucy walked into the room. "Listen for me, will you, so Amity can go for a walk?" Lucy nodded her agreement. "And I heard your aunt. Now, for the last time, go away."

The last strands of red sunset threaded through wispy lines of rising fog. Simon offered his arm because he could not gather her into his embrace. When she linked her arm with his, he placed his hand over hers and closed the distance between them. Relieved she didn't resist the closer contact, he led her toward the moonrise over the river. "I look forward to our walks at the end of the day."

"I do too." She turned her face toward him, her lips slightly upturned. "There is something good about being out here in God's world after being in a carriage all day." Her plaintive tone was not like her usual garrulous manner. She didn't tease or cajole.

Beyond the warehouses on Sophia Street, across the Rappahannock River, a great brick house adorned a small hillock. Its silver-tipped fields waited for spring. A pang for his own fields tugged his chest. "Are you missing home?"

"Maybe a little."

"Are you quite sure you're all right?"

They walked a few steps more past a smaller warehouse. She said nothing but stepped off the street and paused next to a tree to stare out at the river. "I am tired. I am worried for my aunt. But I, myself, am doing well." She paused and took an audible breath before continuing. "When I saw the bear—it is the second time you've come to our rescue on this trip."

The image of the bear rising above her razored through him. Hands on her shoulders he turned her to face him. "When I saw the bear towering over you…"

Her eyes glistened in the fading light. He moved quickly before he decided against himself again. He pressed his lips to hers. She stiffened. He lightened the kiss. She gloriously softened against him. Her hands slid up his arms to thread into his hair. Heart swelling he poured all the waiting, all the relief he felt at her safety into his kiss. A boot scraped on the cobble behind them. He pulled back and tucked her behind his back.

"Miss Amity?"

Amity looked out from behind his elbow.

"There ye are, Miss Amity. I thought t'was ye."

With one hand smoothing her hair, Amity stepped next to him. "Why Mary, whatever are you doing here?"

"Jonathan, that's Daniel's brother, is taking me home, but that's not why I'm here." She pointed to her feet.

What had she seen? He'd promised her father he'd marry her if she'd been compromised. Amity'd probably think he did it on purpose.

"I saw ye walking along the street from my window. I'll not point it out just now being that we have an audience. I thought t'was ye, but I couldn't be sure, so I was taking an extra careful look, and that's when I seen the two gentleman following ye." Simon pulled Amity a little closer.

"Where are they now?" He asked not daring to turn in any direction lest he give Mary away.

"Behind the warehouse two doors down."

"Miss Mary, would you let me have the honor of escorting you home?"

Simon extended his other arm and Mary took it. "If you would show me the way."

She gave him the address one block down from the direction in which they'd just come.

"You must have left at the same time we did. I can't believe we didn't see you on the road."

Simon directed them away from the ordinary.

"We left right after I came back from seeing ye the last time. Jonathan said wind didn't make no difference to soldiers. And I guess he was right. We traveled by horse and slept in our tent."

"So Jonathan did decide to leave."

"His time was up. Said he should be getting back to his parents."

"What will you do?"

They reached the end of Sophia Street, and Simon took them up to Caroline Street to make their way back toward Mary's accommodations.

"I haven't decided for certain, but I think, after we've visited, Danny and me, I think we're going to Bethlehem."

"Pennsylvania?"

"Yes. They've mission work for a woman to do

there. It's time I did something useful for God."

Amity fell silent at Mary's pronouncement.

Simon's heart trembled at what scheme Amity would dream up now. She'd already compromised and settled on Winchester instead of the missions in the Ohio Valley. Would she decide she should follow Mary to the mission field?

They rounded the corner onto Wolfe and approached Blackstone's Tavern.

Amity stopped them and looked around him to Mary. "Would you care to come in for a cup of coffee?"

They settled in the private dining room off the main chamber.

Simon leaned over the table. "Can you describe the men you saw?"

"I only seen them in the shadows, like a camp-cat slinking around after rats. I never seed their faces."

The coffee arrived. Silence fell as they prepared their brews.

17

Winifred fumed behind the door of the private dining parlor. Some thieves. It wasn't like Thomas to choose inept fools. They hadn't struck her as inept either when it came to that, at least the tall one didn't. The less she thought about the short one the better. She pointed and Thomas followed her quietly back to her office.

"They were seen."

"I can't believe I'm going to say this, but in their defense, how could they have known that Morgan would have an ally in a town he's never visited?"

Winifred spun to face him cold fury infused her limbs. "I have no time for incompetence. I can see I shall have to take things into my own hands."

Thomas paled. "Freddie, let me have a talk with them before you put yourself in any danger."

She attempted a laugh. It sounded chilling even to her own ears. "You might have thought of that before you sent me incompetent ruffians. Find them and send them to me."

"Just give me a little more time."

She wavered. "Thomas. The stone is here, right under our noses. We just need to get it." She clenched her fist in desperation as though the stone were already there.

"Surely we have couple of days to procure the stone in such a way that will not put both of you at risk? What kind of life will he have if you are gone?"

Cold stillness stopped her dead. "Two days. I can't afford to wait any longer.

~*~

"If you're ready I shall walk you home, Miss Mary."

Amity stood. "I'll come with you. Give me a minute to check on my aunt." There was no way she would leave Simon to travel home on his own.

Simon frowned. "I think you'd better stay here."

"Your frown won't work on me, Simon Morgan. I will not leave you to walk home alone."

He rolled his eyes at her.

"That won't work either. Those men, whoever they are, left us alone when we were two or three. There is no telling what would happen if one of us travels alone."

"I can walk myself home, Miss Amity. They're not interested in the likes of me."

"Don't be a ninny. Now that you have spent this much time with us, it could be worse for you. It's best we walk together."

"I have to agree with Amity there, Mary. You shouldn't walk alone."

"Then it's settled. Give me a couple of minutes to check on my aunt."

Simon resigned and sat back down.

"Beg your pardon, Miss Amity, but is Miss Clementine ill?"

"I don't know how I didn't think to tell you. She was attacked by a bear."

Mary lost all color. "A bear?"

"He clawed her arm. Simon killed him before he could do anything else."

"And to think I've been traveling with my little Danny all this way."

"I'm sure you've nothing to worry about. It's still too early for bears. I think the mild weather caused that one to rouse early."

"Is there anything I can do to help? I nursed many a soldier…"

"Not at the moment. The doctor has been to see her and re-dressed her arm. Now we just have to wait."

Amity touched her arm to take leave. She found Clementine sleeping soundly. Lucy rocked silently by the bed with her needle weaving in and out of the hem of a red calico dress draped across her lap. Amity nodded to Lucy before closing the door. In the hallway, she bounced off Simon tucking a pistol into his breeches.

"I wish I'd thought of that." Amity whispered. Not that she owned a gun that small. She'd have to look into acquiring one if she was to travel the world as a free woman. She sent up a prayer that they would have no need of it tonight.

Simon grinned and followed her down the narrow

stairs.

Outside, frosty air bit at the exposed skin of her face. She tucked a little closer to Simon's warmth than propriety dictated, but he didn't seem to mind. And there was the matter of the kiss they shared. Once again, she prayed that tonight would end peacefully so a discussion of what that kiss did or didn't mean for their future could take place.

The three of them walked in silence.

Amity scanned the area listening for anything that might be men approaching them.

Mary disappeared into the ordinary where Jonathan and little Danny waited.

Before they reached the corner of Wolfe Street, two men stepped out of the shadows of the warehouse across the street. The man who approached was tall. His companion came up to his shoulder.

"Mr. Morgan?"

Simon stopped and slipped Amity a little behind him on his right.

"Is it Mr. Morgan?"

"Who are you?"

"My name's Oliver Hugh, sir. I have been directed to give you this note from some people who know John Parchment."

"Why didn't he just mail it?"

"The post isn't what it should be is it, sir?"

Simon took the folded paper from Hugh. "Have you been following me all night?"

"We have been waiting to see you alone, yes, sir."

"We did see two other fellas who looked like they

might be interested in ye..." the shorter one spoke his voice raspy.

Amity tightened her grip on his arm and stepped in closer. "What did you see?"

"Not much, sir. But we were told to hang about and make sure no mischief befell ye."

Indeed. Simon tucked the note into his coat pocket. "Thank you, gentlemen."

"We are to wait for a reply."

Simon suppressed the urge to shout at the men for a myriad of things, not the least of which was frightening Amity. "Well, it cannot be read in the dark, can it? Follow me."

"Simon—"

"Later."

Amity bit her tongue and stayed close to his side.

The two men walked a few paces behind them. Amity forced herself to not look back and inquire after them. Who were these strangers, and what could they possibly want with Simon? *What mischief are they protecting us from?*

Bending near a candle in the Tavern's entryway Simon broke the seal. He took slow care with the intricate folds then dropped his arms in frustration.

"Tell the sender I shall meet with him at the designated place."

The two men bowed and left.

Amity stepped close to whisper and forgot what she wanted to say. His closeness brought the kiss they'd shared into sharp memory. He placed his arm around her shoulder to turn into the private parlor away from the gaming in the main chamber. "Simon, what is going on, and who wants to do you mischief?"

"Let's have a seat."

They sat facing each other in front of the small fire.

The small fire illuminated the fine lines beginning to form at his gentle eyes. Funny, she'd never noticed them before. She reached up and smoothed the hair that slipped onto his forehead.

He hesitated to speak.

Did her nearness blank his mind too? A gentle glow of knowing warmed her heart and extended throughout her limbs. She loved him. Ever since she could remember, she'd loved him.

"Amity," he took her hand in both of his.

"Simon, what is this mischief?"

The alarm she felt at him in danger wasn't new. She always worried about him. He could be so lost in his work that he wouldn't come out for days. Someone had to look out for him; he was too trusting.

"I have something to tell you..." He retrieved something from his pocket. He held it a few seconds between his thumb and forefinger before placing it in her hand.

"It is a rock."

"Precisely."

The stone was warm from his pocket and smooth between her thumb and forefinger. "Is this what the mischief is about?"

"I think so."

"But what is it?"

"I am still trying to figure that out."

He sat back in his chair still holding one of her hands. Amity held the stone before the candle on the table; it was a clear green with markings in the middle. "It is beautiful. Where did you get it? Is it some kind of gemstone, like a very large diamond?"

"I hadn't really thought of it like that." He explained how he'd gotten it from the sea captain at Miller's Ordinary, and also John Parchment's and the secret society's interest in the stone. "I was so caught up in its possible supernatural meanings that it never occurred to me it might have some intrinsic value by simply being a large gemstone."

"Who are these so-called important men that have such interest?"

"I don't know yet. John has kept their names from me." He handed her the note. "I suppose they will have to reveal themselves in three days' time."

"I will pray for guidance tonight."

"Thank you." He leaned in and Amity forgot to breathe.

"Simon…" She forced herself to turn away from his kiss.

"I'm sorry." He placed a hand on her arm.

She turned back, stomach churning. "I'm not sorry, Simon." She covered his hand with her own. "But what does it mean?"

Lucy shuffled into the room. "Miss Amity, Miss Clementine is awake and asking for you."

Amity stood. Simon followed, "We will have to talk soon."

~*~

Clementine sat propped by two flattish pillows. "It's rather late, I knew you were walking, but I didn't think you'd try to make it to Winchester on foot." Groggy from the laudanum she hesitated around a dry throat.

"What may I get for you?"

"A cup of tea would be nice."

There was no tea to be had for honest folk. The embargo took care of that. Amity poured a small amount of coffee from the pot into the dish provided.

Clementine took the cup with hands that radiated heat.

Oh no. "Lucy, call for Simon. We need to get Dr. Solomon back tonight."

"You won't need Mr. Simon for that. I saw the doctor not ten minutes ago, down the hallway."

"Then go ask Mr. Burns to send Dr. Solomon whenever—"

The door creaked open, and the round head of the doctor peered in. "Did I hear you call for me, Miss Archer?"

"My aunt has a fever."

The doctor stepped toward the bed. He felt Clementine's forehead and checked her pulse. He unwrapped her arm cleaned it once more and rewrapped it.

"What can I do?"

"There is so much that we don't know."

Sensing the deliberate pause Amity waited.

"I see no infection." He stroked his deep black beard. "We need to keep the wound as clean as humanly possible…some infection may have entered the wound despite our efforts. We usually think of fevers as coming only with infection, but I've begun to think recently that it may be part of the body fighting to live. Much like we get warm when we exercise. It is but a theory of mine with no proof, but I think we shall see her improve in the next twenty-four, maybe forty-eight hours. Try to keep her cool."

"Should we not stoke the fire to keep her warm?"

"I shouldn't think so. Do you like a hot fire on a warm summer day out in the garden?" The right side of his mouth angled up in a half smile.

"Definitely not."

"Let's give her body a chance to do its work." He picked up his bag, took two strides to the door, and spun around with one finger in the air. "And let her have some more of the physic I gave her, it will help."

Amity caught his free right hand. "Thank you, sir."

"I will check in tomorrow."

18

Two days passed while Clementine's fever burned.

Simon busied himself reading. He kept close to the tavern in case Amity or her aunt should need anything. He glimpsed Amity only in passing. If she required anything, she sent a servant. She only left herself when absolutely necessary.

Midway through the third morning Simon caught Amity in the hall outside Clementine's door.

"How is she?"

"She feels warmer to me. I have written to my father, but it is too soon to hear from him." Her stormy eyes sheltered pools of tears. "She is talking to Uncle William as though he sat on the bed next to her." The tears spilled down her checks.

A protective feeling surged through him. Simon gathered her into his arms and placed a kiss upon her head. "Have you eaten?"

"Not yet. I was on my way down." He released her. Fatigue deepened the tiny lines around her eyes.

Mr. Burns escorted them to the private dining parlor. "How does Mrs. Foster this morning?"

"Not much improved, Mr. Burns."

"Shall I send your breakfast upstairs?"

"No," Simon interrupted. "Bring Miss Archer something to eat here." He turned to her. "You need some rest. You can go back after you've eaten."

"I'm not very hungry, Simon." She looked up at Mr. Burns. "I shall need Dr. Solomon today if you can arrange for him to see my aunt."

"I shall do just that. I believe I may catch him before he leaves." The man left.

"There must be something going around. He is here almost every time I think I need him."

"I wondered if you would like to visit Dr. Solomon with me."

A hand flew to her chest. "Are you well?"

"Yes. I'm quite well. I'm going to see him about the stone."

Confusion played across her countenance. "Oh, yes. The gemstone."

"Tonight is my meeting, and I would like to speak to someone who might be able to interpret the writing in the center."

"You think it's writing?"

He waited while the servant placed her food on the table. Once she'd begun to eat, he explained all the theories that he knew to date without telling her of his own experiment and what the stone had meant to him.

"I don't dare leave yet," Amity said when he finished. "I'm distressed being from Aunt Clementine for this long. Perhaps you could see the doctor after he sees my aunt. I don't think I can eat any more." She rose to leave. "Come up when you are ready and maybe you can talk to the doctor then."

Dr. Solomon accompanied Amity out of Aunt Clementine's room and stopped in the hallway. "And still we wait, Miss Archer. I find her pulse strong. Her mind is weakened by fever. It is delirium, nothing else." Dr. Solomon was tall with a round face that made Amity think he worked at staying lean.

"It's just I've heard—"

"That the dead visit the dying?"

Amity nodded her head. Indeed, who hadn't heard of such things?

"I am a man of science Miss Archer. I have not seen ghosts talking to any of my patients. Nor have my patients reported such things to me."

Perhaps they were too afraid to tell you? "Thank you, Dr. Solomon."

"Get some rest, Miss Archer. I don't wish to have another patient under this roof. Two is quite enough." His mouth quirked a bit.

Simon came up to them.

"Dr. Solomon, this is my friend, Simon Morgan. I believe you met the day we arrived."

Simon offered his hand.

"Yes, of course I remember meeting you." Dr. Solomon brought both hands to the handle of his bag.

"Perhaps you would meet me in my room?" Simon asked.

"Sure."

Simon led the doctor to his room and closed the door.

~*~

"How may I assist you?" The doctor asked.

Simon laid the stone on the desk. "Can you read this writing?"

"Where did you pick up such a thing?" Solomon picked up the stone and smoothed it between thumb and forefinger, then cast it up to the light at the window.

Once again, Simon told his story.

"It is ancient writing, but I think I understand it." He put the stone back on the desk. "I am not permitted to say this name out loud. But it is a name of the God of Israel. Do you know what it is?"

"I am not sure. I have been told that it might be one of the stones from the back of the breastplate."

He smiled at that. "I am a doctor—not a rabbi—but if I remember my history correctly, those things are lost to history. There is some speculation that it wasn't present at the time of the Second Temple, so I sincerely doubt their presence here now."

Simon cleared his throat. "Can you tell me what you know about the Horeb stone?"

"I don't know about anything called a Horeb stone. I thought you were speaking of the Urim and Thummim."

Simon nodded his head in agreement. "I was told this stone might be one of them."

"You will need a rabbi who has studied the priestly garments. I'm not sure that scholarship exists in the colonies. Have you a piece of paper? I will give you a name and a direction."

Simon handed over a small sheet of foolscap.

Dr. Solomon scratched a quill across and handed it back. "Perhaps this man can help you."

Upon exiting the room, they found Amity waiting in the corridor next to her aunt's open room. "Dr. Solomon, I have one more quick question."

"Yes?" His surprisingly deep voice still soft.

"Can you recommend a lawyer in Fredericksburg?"

"I have only had dealings with my own people."

"I have no issue with your people, Dr. Solomon."

"The man I recommend is honest. You may tell him that I sent you." He scratched across the bottom of Simon's foolscap and handed it to him.

"Thank you."

"You are most welcome. I will check on your aunt later." His smile lightened all his features and Simon thought he could do worse than call him friend.

"Your father didn't mention that you would need a lawyer." Simon eyed her.

"He probably didn't have time as I only found out myself the morning we left."

"May I ask why you need to see a lawyer?"

~*~

The need to share her plans had become a burden. With Clementine so sick, they had lost much time. Simon would have to get back to planting. Sitting with her aunt had given her time to form list after list of things that should be done for Lucy and her freedom, half of which she would never have time to do. It looked as though their trip to Winchester would not happen after all. If that is what God decided would be, then she would have to be content with that, but that didn't mean she couldn't free Lucy. She had to find a way to get Lucy out of Virginia safely.

And that was easier said than done. None of the plantation owners she knew was keen on having freed slaves around. Aside from Field and her father, she wasn't sure members of her own family would approve. Not that it mattered. Lucy, her best friend from childhood, deserved this, and Amity would make certain it happened, no matter the cost. She said a small prayer that her answer would come soon. "I haven't even told Aunt Clementine, although she's probably figured it out. She's like that."

Simon nodded a small smile creasing his cheeks.

"I cannot speak of it openly. Perhaps if we find a quiet place to sit?"

"Someone recently told me that he believes he has more privacy out walking on the street than in a quiet coffee shop where the walls have ears."

Amity shivered then straightened her spine. "I'm not afraid." She linked their arms and chose her words carefully. "Lucy has bought her freedom."

"Indeed?"

"Yes. My father recommended that I see a lawyer for the correct papers. And I think he should view the transaction as well. I do not want Lucy to have to watch her back her whole life."

"I will go with you."

"I cannot leave until Aunt Clementine is out of the

wilderness, as Dr. Solomon says."

"Then I will bring the lawyer to you."

Hope rose in her heart. How had she not thought of that? She must be more tired than she realized. Of course they could do the business here. Amity handed over the torn paper she'd gotten from Dr. Solomon.

"I shall be back directly."

~*~

Glad to be doing something productive Simon stepped out in the street in search of Joseph Moses's establishment in Sophia Street. The stone in his pocket had become a permanent fixture to the end that he no longer knew if it grew warm or cold. The pistol residing in his other pocket was cold.

Thanks to Dr. Solomon's introduction, it took less than one minute of persuasion to procure Mr. Moses's promise to follow him to the Blackstone Tavern.

"You have caught me at a very opportune time as I was closing up for the day. I shall have time to follow you to meet this Miss Archer and discover how I may be of assistance."

The dandy little man barely reached Simon's shoulder. Dressed in fine black cloth and a sculpted coat, Simon stopped short of asking after his tailor.

Sophia Street, on the banks of the Rappahannock River, boasted tall wooden warehouses no doubt still full of goods meant for England. Dusk made fuzzy lines of the structures. Lengthened shadows crept across the street. Camp-cats, Mary had called the men following them that night. Simon glanced around the street. He wondered if she watched now or if she and her brother-in-law had left for Winchester. Simon took hold of the pistol in his pocket.

A man yanked Moses from his side.

A vice grip grabbed Simon's right arm from behind. "What's a fine—" Simon wrenched his right arm and grabbed the shoulder of the man's thin coat, dislodged the man's grip, and swung his left hand around and pointed his gun into the hollow of the man's cheek.

A quick glance at Moses's showed his assailant in the same position.

"What do you want?"

"Nothin' mister," the short one whined.

"Just let us go. We'll not bother ye again."

"The magistrate is in the next block." Moses offered.

~*~

A soft tap at the door roused Amity from her chair next to her aunt.

"Mary?"

"I left Danny with Jon and I came as soon as I could, Miss Amity."

"I saw Mr. Simon attacked in the street along with a little man I never seen before. He was quick for so little a fellow. They stopped them thieves in their tracks. It was the same two men from the other night. Then they took 'em off. I guess they went to the jail. I thought I should tell ye."

Amity's stomach seized. "Is he all right?"

"By the way he marched the attacker off I think so." Mary laid her hand on Amity's arm. "How is Miss Clementine?"

"Still with a fever."

"If you would permit me, I have an old family recipe for a fever. I can bring it later if ye like."

"I'll try anything."

"Don't forget the blanket, Willie, you'll freeze…"

Amity wrung out a cloth and placed it on her aunt's forehead. "She's been doing that all day."

"She'll be all right, Miss Amity. It's just the fever."

"I have heard of folks talking to the dead before they die."

"No, Miss Amity. They don't talk to them. They see them. It's different." Mary adjusted the blanket covering Clementine. "I remember one young soldier told me his mother come to see him home. She's right over there he said, pointing to the corner of the tent." Mary fanned herself with flattened hands. "He was so young. Later that morning he went, as peaceful as could be."

Amity lifted a stray tendril and placed it carefully out of the way of the cloth.

"She's not said anything like that."

"I've seen it more than once. They will tell ye 'me old Dad came and laid down with me last night'. Those people are awake, not delirious with fever like she is. Rest yourself, miss. It's just the fever talking is all."

A small knot of peace began to unravel the despair

that had twisted Amity's guts since daybreak. Amity placed a hand on her friend's arm. "It must have been so hard."

"If I ever serve in a hospital again, it will be too soon." She patted Amity's hand. "I'd best get back and make that special tea."

~*~

It was full dark by the time the would-be thieves were incarcerated, and Simon and the lawyer finally ascended the steps of the tavern.

"You must allow me to buy your supper." Simon offered.

"On the contrary. You have done me a very great service. If I had gone to the magistrate alone, the man who attacked me would be free on the street."

"Surely not."

"It has happened to me before, my friend." He held open the door. "Now tell me what I can do to help you while I buy you something to eat and drink."

Mr. Burns pulled a face when seating the two men in the private dining chamber. One look from Simon and the man snapped to attention. "What may I bring you gentlemen?"

Moses ordered the finest meat and vegetables the tavern had to offer along with a bottle of their most expensive brandy. "There is a small matter I wish to discuss with you before we get to our original business." Moses said while cutting into his beef.

"Oh?"

"Fredericksburg is still a very small town. We have a collection of worthies, most with the surname of Washington, but essentially it is still fairly small." He lifted his glass to his lips. "Tomorrow you have agreed to meet with a small set of us. Let me assure you that you have friends. Assessments must be made before you are brought into the fold."

"What fold?"

"We are a small group of men committed to a set of ideals."

"And what might those be?"

"We can speak more in depth at another time. I'm sure you understand the need for circumspection. These are dangerous times, as our adventure this evening proves."

"To tell you the truth, Mr. Moses…"

"Joseph, please."

"Joseph. I grow weary of these games. I have come into possession of a rock. Many people are interested in my rock." He pulled it from his pocket and smoothed it. "I could just sell it to the highest bidder."

Joseph's shrewd eyes watched the stone.

"But I find I'm attached to it in some odd way. I don't wish to part with it." He closed it in his palm. "And I don't think I shall."

"That is, of course, your right." Joseph's dark eyes twinkled in the candlelight. "But surely it's worth it to you to discover its value—if it has any—and I'm fairly certain you know it does."

Simon slipped the stone securely into his pocket.

Joseph's eyes never left Simon's.

"I brought you here to meet with a young lady."

Joseph stopped smiling.

Simon called for a boy to request Amity to come down.

19

Another soft tap revealed a servant requesting her presence downstairs.

"I will stay with Miss Clementine, Miss Amity."

"I shall return directly."

The two men stood when Amity entered the chamber.

"Miss Archer." Mr. Moses stepped away from the table and bowed. There is nothing to fear, she told her quaking insides.

"Mr. Moses it is kind of you to come so late in the day."

He inclined his head slightly, "You are most welcome. How may I be of assistance?"

"Mr. Moses, I wish you to witness the fact that my slave, Lucy, has purchased her freedom."

"Is Lucy here with you?"

"Yes, of course."

"I shall go find her." Simon excused himself from the room.

"Shall we sit down?" Mr. Moses waved her to a seat. He waited for her to take her place before he resumed his seat. "This is not something I see every day." He took a sip from his cup. "But it is a fairly simple transaction."

Simon returned with a flustered Lucy and Jax with a grin wide enough to brighten the entire room.

Mr. Moses did not stand when Lucy entered the room. "Please have a seat." He directed her to the chair next to Amity's. "Now Lucy, you understand that once you have gained your freedom you must leave Virginia?"

"Yes, sir, I understand that."

"Well, if I'm to witness, let me see the money."

Lucy reached into her pocket and placed a rolled handkerchief filled with coins on the table in front of Amity.

Amity opened the cloth and counted. "It is sufficient."

Mr. Moses took note of the ten pounds.

"I shall have my clerk draw up a more formal paper tomorrow. You may both come and sign tomorrow afternoon."

Amity glanced from Mr. Moses to Lucy. "Is that all there is?"

"Essentially, yes. It will not be official until you both sign the document tomorrow." He smiled at them both.

"Miss Amity, is he serious? I'm free?"

Amity looked at Mr. Moses once more. He nodded his head vigorously smiling all the while.

Lucy stood up and stepped away from the table.

Amity stood.

Lucy looked at the floor and gave her usual curtsy. "Miss Amity, I think I need to go for a walk or something."

"Miss Lucy."

Lucy looked up.

Amity curtsied.

Lucy's eyes filled. Jax took her by the hand.

"Perhaps I shall see you when you return. We have a few things we should discuss, if you think you will have the time."

"Miss Amity, I will always have time for you."

She dropped Jax's hand and grabbed Amity into an embrace reminiscent of the ones they'd shared as children.

Amity's heart swelled with peace. She'd done the right thing. Deep inside something off kilter set itself straight, clean, and unburdened.

Lucy and Jax disappeared outside hand in hand.

When the door closed behind them, a loud squeal sounded outside the tavern.

Simon and Mr. Moses were deep in conversation when she returned.

"I shall provide them a wagon," Simon spoke with a smile.

"But they will need a sizable stake to set up house in Ohio. It's not exactly the right time to leave either. There are no crops in the field."

"I'm sure Jax has thought of that, but I'm prepared to set them up. If they hurry and find a suitable place, they can get crops in the ground in time. The Ohio season will be a bit behind ours."

Amity returned to the table quietly heart in her throat. How like him to be so generous.

She sent him a small wave and headed back up to

179

her aunt and Mary.

"Jonathan says the weather's cleared up enough for us to be on our way."

"We will see you before you leave?" Amity asked.

"I be bringing the tea in the morning for Miss Clementine. I'd better get back and inform him of that. He still moves like the army. Up ye go and off ye go with no warning to the troops. Only now it's me and Danny that's troops." She laughed at her own joke

After penning a letter to her father updating Clementine's condition, Amity settled into a chair she'd placed next to the bed what seemed like years ago…but in reality was just three days.

A soft tapping of her hand woke her in the night. No moon shown in the window and the candle had long gone out.

"Is that you, Amity?"

Amity grasped the cool hand of Clementine.

"Oh, Aunt Clementine, your hand is so cool."

A deep intake of breath and slow exhale. "I think I feel better."

Amity lit the candle.

Clementine pushed herself up with her one good arm. Though pale and a little thinner, the twinkle returned to her eye. "I'm famished. What did you save me to eat?"

Amity grinned and brought her a dish of broth and small piece of bread.

"Not bad." She said after a sip of the cold liquid. "William did know his taverns."

"That he did." After Clementine ate a little more,

she grew tired.

Amity blew out the light and stretched out on one of the servant's beds. She closed her eyes and didn't open them until a soft tap played on the door.

Mary arrived with Danny on her hip and a tankard of tea.

"Oh, Danny, I didn't know you were in Fredericksburg too!" Aunt Clementine held out her good arm.

Mary let him down on the side of the bed. "If you're sure?"

"I'm positive." Clementine gave Danny a little squeeze. "Now what's this you've brought me?"

"It's an old family recipe. It's a tea to help with the fever." Mary touched Clementine's hand. "Which you don't have."

"It broke in the night."

"Well, it won't hurt you to have a dish of tea anyway."

Mary poured and Clementine drank.

"It's not like any tea I've ever tasted."

"I didn't say it tasted good, I said it was good medicine."

The three women laughed and settled in for a good visit since it might be the last time they might get the chance.

"Be sure to leave me your direction so I may look you up when next I travel to Winchester." She glanced at Amity, "I don't think I will make it this time."

There. It was said out loud. Amity's dream blackened. She wouldn't make it to the mountains after all.

"I think, Miss Clementine, you should give me your direction. I'm not staying in Winchester long. I plan to go to the mission towns."

Clementine said nothing. She took a long look at Mary. "It's a hard job, but you've seen worse." She reached for Mary. "God bless you, and your child…"

"I must go where He calls me. I've felt this calling for some time now."

"Then you must go. Amity will write my direction for you, and you let me know if you need anything."

"Yes, ma'am."

"I am sincere, Mary. I cannot come with you, but if I can help you, write to me and I'll send what I can."

"Me, too." Amity chimed in handing Mary a paper with both Clementine's and her directions. "Let us hear from you often. I'll need to know where to send your copy of the book."

Mary's eyes lit. "Oh, yes, I'd nearly forgotten."

Amity closed the door for their guests and turned to find Clementine's shrewd eyes focused on her.

"It's time you got some rest and cleaned up." Her aunt instructed.

Amity touched her hair and ran a hand down her stomacher. A bath would be lovely. She grinned. "I could say the same for you."

"Call for Matilda. She will help me."

After a bath and donning a clean dress of blue cotton. Amity felt ready to answer the message sent by Mr. Moses that Lucy's papers were ready for their signatures. She found Lucy downstairs with Simon in the private parlor dressed in her red cotton standing tall next to Jax. "Are we ready then?"

A crisp sunshine met them on the porch. The temperature had dropped since the previous day, and Amity was glad of her woolen cloak. Jax took the lead with Lucy on his arm. Amity was glad to follow on Simon's. Lucy walked down the street head high. She and Jax whispered to each other like the other couples they passed. Amity knew it wouldn't be as easy as this short walk was turning out to be, but today she would take it as presentment of a happy future for her friend.

Mr. Moses met them at the door and escorted them into his small office. The men remained standing in the background as Amity and Lucy conducted their business. Moses looked surprised that Lucy could sign her name.

"Miss Amity has always been my friend." She glanced at Amity sitting beside her. "I can say that now."

Eyes filled with tears they held hands.

Mr. Moses slid their copies of the papers across his desk.

"I wish you peace and happiness, Miss Lucy."

"Thank you, Mr. Moses. I wish you the same."

They left and went straight back to the tavern.

"I'm gonna put my paper in a safe place. I don't want to lose it while we's shopping this afternoon."

Amity followed Lucy up to their room. She took a seat on the bed while Lucy placed her paper in her satchel.

"Lucy, may I have a word?"

Lucy sat next to Amity.

Amity reached across and took Lucy's hand.

"I hope you can forgive me...I didn't..." She didn't know how to say that she'd never realized her childhood friend was a slave and all that it entailed. Kept against her will, made to work... "I don't have the words, Lucy."

"Amity, you are my friend. You are forgiven. There's all kinds of trouble in this world, and you did your part to make it right. The light is shining out from under your bushel."

Lucy held out her arms, and Amity rested in her embrace. Amity had done something right, but how had she not seen what was wrong in the first place? She had a lot of thinking to do. Amity placed the ten pounds into Lucy's hands. "I will give you more before you leave. I'm waiting to hear from my father."

"Mr. Simon told Jax he'd give him a stake so we can buy us some land in Ohio."

"I know, but I want you to know that you can write to me if you need anything. I will send help as I can."

"Thank you, Miss Amity."

"I will have to come and see your babies."

Lucy blushed. "It's time you were thinking about babies of your own."

"You may be right. I had thought that time was past, but I used to think I knew a lot of things that I'm not so certain about now."

"I've seen the way Mr. Simon looks at you. Has looked at you for years."

Amity could no longer deny the love she felt for him. Whether it would work out, she didn't know. The opportunity to discuss the kiss that highlighted her dreams hadn't been possible while her aunt burned with fever. Perhaps tonight.

"We'll just have to wait and see."

20

Simon arrived in the private dining chamber a few minutes before seven. He chose a spot at the table that would allow him to clearly see the faces of all the men John invited. At John Parchment's arrival with a more somberly dressed Roger White. Mrs. Blackstone swirled in wearing a fashionable cotton gown of a crimson that leant warmth to her porcelain complexion.

"Mrs. Blackstone, I had heard this was your tavern, but I've not seen you these few days we've stayed here."

"Good evening, Mr. Morgan. I hope you do not feel slighted, I have been frightfully busy since my return, but I had to stop for a very few minutes to greet the husband of my oldest and dearest friend." She extended her hand to John who bowed over it.

"No offense taken." Simon bowed. In fact, he was quite pleased he'd not had to deal with her, their last encounter being less than pleasant.

Other guests arrived on the heels of John and White. Mrs. Blackstone stayed long enough to be introduced to Mr. Cason Dawley, a severe man, tall and gaunt; Mr. Joel Singleton also tall, but he hadn't missed many meals; and Mr. Dennis Cornick a short trim man when compared to the other two was very ordinary indeed; before declaring herself terribly busy and departing in swirl of crimson.

"Gentleman." Simon bowed to the men and waved to seats for them all.

John closed the door behind him.

Silence reigned until tankards arrived for each of the men. Dawley nodded to John to close the door.

"Now that we are alone, I think we can begin." He glanced around the table for agreement and leaned onto his forearms resting not the table. Simon sat back in his chair. "Mr. Morgan, let me begin by telling you how much we appreciate your time."

Simon inclined his head.

"Might we see the stone?" Greedy eyes and bobbing heads circled the table.

Reluctance stiffened his fingers and straightened his back.

"Before I do that, I should like to understand exactly your interest in the stone."

"We believe it might be the Horeb stone."

"Yes. I've heard that, what exactly does the Horeb stone do for you?"

Dawley looked around the table once again. Simon followed his glance and took in puzzled looks.

"You mean you don't know?" Cornick asked in a hoarse whisper.

"Not in the least." Frustration raised Simon's normally even tone.

"Please, keep your voice down." Dawley made downward movements with boney hands.

"The Horeb stone will allow the user to ask questions of God."

"Gentleman, I hardly think that a little stone will let you talk to God."

Movement rustled through the men. Obviously, they did not agree. Simon reached for the stone in his pocket.

"If we may see, perhaps we can make that determination." Dawley nearly salivated. Beads of sweat popped out on his overly large brow. He had to stop himself from rubbing his hands together.

"Mr. Moses, you're a Jew. You cannot believe this is true."

"There are many things in the world that people know little about, Simon. Powerful things."

Simon reached into his pocket. Cool to the touch, the stone sat in the palm of his hand as if it belonged there.

"I will place it on the table. I request that you ask before you touch it in any way."

"Mr. Morgan, we did not come to steal the stone, only to observe it."

"The rule stands."

The rest of them nodded their agreement.

"Very well."

Simon placed his fist over the center of the table and slowly released the stone from fingers still stiffened by reluctance.

Roger White stood. "It's not the same stone."

"I assure you it is."

"It's not the same color."

"That has happened one time before."

"You mean it has changed color?" Dawley's chair creaked as he shifted forward.

"Yes, it is also cooler to the touch. I am sure it will return to normal after you gentleman depart."

"How can you be certain?"

"It is what happened the last time."

"May I?" Roger White kept his hands folded on the table in front of him waiting.

"Yes."

Boney fingers lifted the stone from the table. "It's as cold as the winter wind."

"What did it look like before?" Singleton asked, never taking his eyes from the muddy green stone White held to the candle near him.

"It was clear green like an aquamarine." White spoke in an awed whisper, "The writing looks the same."

"When you are finished you may place the stone back on the table." Simon ordered. "After he puts it down, Mr. Moses, I would like you to take a look at the writing."

Joseph picked up the stone and held it to the candle flame. "Roger is right; it is cold." He stared at the center of the stone. "I am not permitted to say His name, but it is our people's name for the God of Israel." Joseph put the stone back on the table. A thoughtful expression replaced the usual twinkle in his dark eyes.

Singleton picked it up next. He agreed it was cold and placed it back on the table clearly not impressed.

John declined a turn. Dawley placed it between his thumb and forefinger and tested its smoothness. Before Simon could declare enough, Dawley put it back on the table.

"Mr. Morgan"--Dawley sat back in his much protesting chair-- "Are you available to meet with us again tomorrow night?"

Simon did not take his eyes of the stone. "Is tonight not enough?"

"We would like to evaluate the stone in a more formal setting."

Simon palmed the stone and placed it back where it belonged.

~*~

"Come and sit by me." Clementine patted the space on the bed.

Amity closed her journal and sat next to her aunt.

"Are you sorry to go home without seeing those mountains?"

Amity picked the edge of her mantua pushing down her disappointment. "Yes. I am disappointed, but it's been a glorious trip—aside from your mishap—" She felt herself redden.

Clementine chuckled deep and took Amity's hand. "Good. I wouldn't expect anything else."

Amity searched her aunt's eyes. "I shouldn't be so selfish."

"Feeling disappointment isn't selfish. It's what you do with it that matters."

"I shall have to think about that for a while, I think."

"You do that, but after you tell me about your Mr. Morgan. I don't imagine you have seen much of him since I have been ill."

"No, I haven't. I've been here with you."

"I may not be your mother, but I can tell when something is going on, so you better just tell me."

The glow she felt every time she thought of the kiss they shared warmed her middle and radiated out to all her limbs. Amity grinned. "I don't want to read too much into it…" The boldness, an ever-ready part of her nature fled she knew not where.

"He kissed you then?"

Her discomfort deepened as her face flushed.

"And about time too." Glee beamed from every crease in Clementine's visage. Dreams of hazel-eyed babies and slow walks in the evenings intruded into the candle-lit room.

"I thought I would never marry."

"Why ever would you think such a thing?"

"I decided when I was a young girl that I would not marry unless I could be as happy as my parents—and you and Uncle William—"

"We were very happy."

"Yes, but not everyone of our acquaintance is so blessed in their marriages."

"True, and though William and I were very happy, what your parents have…I've never seen their like."

"And when Simon didn't love me as I loved him, I knew I would have to find someone else to love…and I never did."

Clementine reached for her hand.

"Simon Morgan loves you, child. And if I am not mistaken, it is not a new feeling for him."

"We have not had a chance to speak alone together these past few days. Hopefully, we will have the chance before we leave for home."

"Give him time…he is likely being careful out of respect for me. Now that I am better, I think you will see him move much more quickly indeed."

"I hope you are right."

"Of course I'm right. And tomorrow I'm getting out of this bed and going downstairs to eat a proper meal."

~*~

Winifred stepped silently away from the door to the private dining chamber to her room. Tomorrow night Dawley and the others would take possession of the stone; there was no doubt of that. Through the crack in the adjoining door, she gazed at her son. Steady deep breaths filled his room. She closed the door gently.

An oval framed pencil sketch she'd made of Charlie while they were courting hung on the wall next to her looking glass. A flirty smile and an appraising eye met her gaze.

"Not tonight, Charlie." She focused her attention to her own face. Severity replaced the plump softness Charlie had admired. Definitely not the girl she'd been when she married Charlie Blackstone. "Enough." She told herself eye to eye as she released her long black hair to fall in soft curls about her shoulders. "Better." A little rouge. "Better, still." She unpinned her stomacher placing the pins in the little dish Charlie bought when... "Enough." Her finest chemise, most delicate robe, and slippers. She stood again in front of the glass. "Even better."

All she had to do was wait.

~*~

Amity left her aunt with a promise of getting out of bed in the morning. She tiptoed into her room hoping not to wake Lucy who must be sleeping soundly by now.

"I'm awake, Miss Amity."

"No more "miss", just Amity."

"I can't believe it's real. So many things happening all at once."

Amity sat on the edge of her own bed. Lucy rolled to face her on her bed next to the opposite wall.

"I confess I didn't know you had an understanding with Jax."

"I won't say it was an understanding exactly...well, maybe that is what it was. I often wondered why he didn't leave when Master Morgan freed him, but we never talked about it until yesterday. Then he told me he was waiting for me."

A bubbly warmth filled Amity overflowing into a grin. "I'm so happy for you."

Lucy grinned back. Amity was reminded of their childhood conspiracies.

"Do you remember those cookies your mama used to bake when the weather got cold and we couldn't play outside?" Amity asked.

"Hmmm."

"Your mama makes the best food I ever ate." Cold thread weaved into the warmth of happiness. "What do you want me to tell your mama?"

"Tell her I'll be back for her."

"Lucy, I—" Amity bit back her words. She couldn't betray her father's trust not even this once. It could mean that Lucy would never be reunited with her mama.

"What is it Miss Amity?"

"Nothing. I will tell your mama that you are coming. And I'll tell Papa that you plan to do so. That way he'll be ready." Flickering candlelight danced on the floor between them. "You will write to me and let me know how you are doing?"

"Of course I will. Did you see Mr. Moses' face when he saw me write my name?"

Fits of giggles and many reminisces later Amity stood and wrapped a shawl around her shoulders. "Are you ready for tomorrow?"

"As ready as I'm gonna be."

Amity excused herself and made her way down to the necessary.

21

Light still rimmed Amity's door when Simon approached his own room. He felt the stone resting in his pocket, had it returned to its normal color? Ultimately, it did not matter. Finally, after years of waiting, the woman he wanted, dreamed of for ten years, was nearly his. There were so many things yet to be discovered. Who was he to say that young Tom was wrong? Since owning the stone, he did indeed have what he always wanted. At least he was closer than he'd ever been. He never thought he'd see the day he'd hold Amity Archer in his arms. He would attend the meeting with Dawley and the others tomorrow night, but they would be sorely disappointed if they thought he'd give up the stone now.

He closed the door quietly behind him and pulled off his coat. What a luxury to have a room to oneself in a tavern. He wrestled the knot at his throat and collapsed into the chair under the window next to his bed. His leather paper case rested on the tabletop. Time to record the events of the evening. Someday, he would tell their children about the stone and how it brought their parents together.

Limbs sprawled he rested his head and closed his eyes.

A creak in the hallway caused him to sit up. Best begin before he found himself in the morning stiff in the chair.

A key slipped into the lock of his door.

Simon drew his pack toward his chair.

The lock clunked open.

He reached for his rifle.

The doorknob turned.

A white figure slipped in through the small crack of the door. Simon lowered his rifle as he straightened to his full height. Winifred Blackstone, clad in a lacy shift and delicate robe, turned to face him after locking the door once more.

"What are you doing?"

Her expression blanked as if he caught her by surprise. The smirk returned quickly. She took a step toward him.

"I thought that would be obvious."

"You can't be serious."

She came close enough for their knees to touch.

Simon stood.

She placed her palms on his chest and let them slowly rise.

He arrested her progress by removing her hands.

"It's all right, Simon. I'm a widow. No one will ever know."

She took his hands by the wrist and placed them on her waist.

Simon removed his hands.

Hands on his waist slid down his thighs.

"Stop."

Porcelain skin glowed in the candlelight. This time, she took his hand and placed it just above her waist, and leaned in for a kiss.

"I said, stop."

He grabbed her arm and stepped her to the door.

~*~

Amity stepped quietly down the hall so not to disturb any other guests before she remembered that they were the only guests. Mumbled voices leaked from Simon's room. Puzzled she moved quickly by to ensure that she didn't overhear what could be going on. She placed her hand on the doorknob of her own room when Winifred Blackstone emerged from Simon's door wearing a chemise and robe. Frozen she watched the woman pass her with that odd sort of smile she always wore.

Amity pushed into her room. Humiliation waved through her. He had said they were friends. Thank God she hadn't approached the subject of the kiss they'd shared. How naive and simple she was.

Her father had been right all along. If Simon had wanted her, he would have offered for her years ago.

Amity pushed herself off the door. Lucy's deep, rhythmic breaths the only sounds in the dark room. Amity craved home. She could walk outside at home. Here she was trapped inside one little room after another.

Trembling fingers struggled to light the candle. Amber light pushed away the darkness. Lucy rolled toward the wall. Amity paced the floor muffling the sound by traveling on the balls of her feet. She needed to go bed. Sleep too lofty a goal for this night. All she wanted to do was crawl to the farthest corner under the bed and hide. How would she ever talk to him again?

She retrieved her night shift from her trunk. Tears dripped on to her stomacher as she tried to focus on her pins. One of them stabbed her shaking finger.

She grabbed her cloak and pattens and slipped back into the hallway.

Drizzle and bone aching cold wrapped wispy tentacles through small gaps in her cloak. The streets of Fredericksburg didn't compare well with the fields of home, but it would have to do. She looked up to the black sky and took in a lung-full of cold air. Then Amity began to walk. She kept to the grassy edges on the roadside to keep out of the slimy pudding of mud the road had become. She walked every street seeing nothing but dying dreams.

Light still shown from the main dining chamber the second time she passed the tavern. She continued on to the next corner and found her eyes had dried, and her head began to rein in her heart.

Hopefully, the roads would be passible tomorrow. If not, they could leave the day after tomorrow. Aunt Clementine was eager to get out of bed. She turned at the corner of the street to head back toward the tavern. It wasn't wise to go too far without Simon to protect her.

Another wave of embarrassment crested in her

heart. She would have to tell Clementine. If only she had not gone on about never loving anyone else. At least she hadn't waxed on about the children she'd dreamed up in the golden candlelight. Children with hazel eyes and his wide smile cuddling next to her while she read to them the latest adventure she'd written would remain her secret. It was time to go back. She still couldn't sleep, but she thought she could at least lie down and wait until morning. A gust of wind ruffled her cloak brushing out the warmth she'd generated.

She reached the other corner. A cold hand seized her elbow from behind. A tall man stepped into her path. "What have we here, then?" She wasn't sure which of them spoke. She wrestled her arm, but the man held firm and took her other elbow.

The man behind her pressed his body into her back. She raised her shoulders to exclude the intrusion of his face at the base of her neck.

"Give me your money."

The last of her funds lay in her pocket. "I do not have any money."

"Anybody who gives their slaves away gots money and a lot of it. Check your pocket." The tall man stepped in closer. A cloud of brandied fumes burned her nose. She pulled her right arm. Nothing.

"If she don't got any money, boss, she's still got something I want."

Amity planted her feet and wrenched her body. The man lifted her off her feet closing the minuscule space between them.

"I can't check my pocket without the use of my arms."

"Put her down."

Her feet hit the ground. The man released her right arm but kept his hand on her elbow.

Please God, let this be enough. She pulled her arm underneath her cloak.

The man followed the movement of her arm. "I always thought pockets was very interesting things." He rubbed his hand further and further down her arm toward her hand.

"Stop touching me."

"Zeke." The tall man commanded. Zeke dropped his hand from her right arm.

Thank you, Lord. Her fingers curled around her last five dollars. She raised her gaze to the tall man. "I will give you what I have, but you have to agree to let me go."

"That depends on how much ye have." Zeke closed the gap between them again.

Amity stepped away from him and looked at the tall man in front of her.

"Agreed." He focused on his partner. "Let her go, Zeke."

"Ye don't know how much she got yet."

"Let her go."

"Get over there next to him." Amity pointed to the tall man. The tall man nodded slightly. Zeke let her left arm drop and moved toward his partner. Amity pulled her right arm out slowly while grabbing her skirt with her left.

She held out her hand and let the money drop on the ground, turned, and ran as fast as she could back to the tavern. She heard footsteps pound behind her.

"Zeke!"

Amity made the porch without hindrance. Conversations buzzed out to the porch from the gamers still occupying tables in the main chamber.

The street was empty when she took a look from the dining parlor. She peered into the main dining chamber at the men playing cards. Some laughed. Some serious. None noticed her. Not even the always attentive Mr. Burns. She could see his shoulder sitting at his desk in a small office at the back of the room. A cold realization hit her gut. She could have been carried off, and no one would have known until the morning.

Shaking she climbed the narrow steps to her room. If her mother were there, Amity would have climbed into her bed and stayed there until she felt better.

Lucy's breathing still resonated in their room.

Amity slipped out of her dress and donned her nightclothes. She blew out her candle and lay still under the heavy blanket. Uncontrollable shivers wracked her small frame. Then the memory of being in Simon's arms came unbidden. His kiss still made her warm all over. Stupid woman. Tears rolled down the corners of her eyes.

Whatsoever things are true...whatsoever things are honest...whatsoever things are just...if there be any virtue, if there be any praise, think on these things...

The gentle reminder came softly to her heart.

Her love was gone.

Her money was gone.

Distant laughter rose through the tavern to laugh at her.

If there be any praise...she searched her brain. The long fields at home. Acres of planted fields that belonged to her father. Acres that she could roam at will and write her stories.

When I get home, I'm going to take one of my old romps. I'll pack a lunch and be gone all day. No one will know where I am, and I can write. A shadow shivered into her plan.

No, she wouldn't.

22

Simon woke up in his bed alone and irritated. What did she mean by making herself free with the keys and coming into his room? He'd slept with one eye open all night. He washed his face and made his way downstairs to eat. Hopefully, she would keep her distance from him today as she had done for the entirety of the trip until last night.

When he entered the room, John Parchment and Roger White were seated at the table.

"John." Simon offered his hand. Roger White, his mouth full of food, raised the corners of his mouth in a greeting though he stood he still clutched his napkin in his hand. Simon waved his hand for them to sit. "Please don't let me interrupt you. I only came for breakfast."

"We were speaking of the meeting tonight. Shall we all attend together? I believe it's a short walk from here."

"I don't believe I will attend after all."

The boy arrived with a dish of coffee and the diet.

Simon ordered ham, sausage, eggs, and bread.

"Simon surely you realize—" Roger placed a warning hand on John's arm before closing the door. John lowered his voice to a whisper. "Surely you realize the importance of the stone."

Simon glanced at him. "No. I can't say that I do. At least, not what importance it has to you or Dawley and the rest."

"The stone has come to light again after being lost to the ages. There must be a reason. We think that reason is the founding of this new nation. Whoever wields the stone has access to God."

So, there it was. Access to God. Of all the ridiculous things, "I've been carrying around the stone for a couple of weeks now. It has changed color and been warm. That is it, and we don't know if the rock itself isn't responsible for those things." They didn't need to know that God's name lit up when electrified. They also didn't need to know that it might glow.

John and White looked at each other as if neither knew how to proceed.

"Look, God could give the stone to whomever He wanted to. He gave it to me. It's mine." A thought niggled in his spirit that it wasn't quite true, but he was sure it didn't belong to a handful of power-hungry politicians.

Roger White cleared his throat. "This is bigger than you and your little problems—"

Simon stood and picked up his plate. "I'm done talking."

John glanced down at the remains of his breakfast.

Simon took a seat at an empty table next to a window in the main chamber. He requested a newspaper and a fresh dish of coffee. Clouds obscured the patch of sky visible from his window. The ground appeared wet. An oxcart rolled heavily down the street as he wondered if the road was too wet for travel. Looked like Jax and Lucy would be able to leave today as planned. Clementine was better. He'd taken care of John and his friends. All he had left was to speak to Amity about their future.

~*~

Amity woke with crusty eyes. A fire crackled in the fireplace. Lucy was already up and gone from their room. Her bag and other belongings were gone from below her bed.

A deep breath later Amity sat on the edge of the bed. Footsteps in the hall entered her aunt's room. Amity moved quickly through her morning routine so she could make it to her aunt in time to help her out of bed.

Clementine, fully dressed for the day, perched on the edge of her bed when Amity entered the room.

"Aunt Clementine you are up!"

Dr. Solomon stood grinning next to her aunt clearly prepared to help her exit her convalescence.

"Of course I'm up. I told you I wasn't staying in this bed one minute longer than I have to." She reached for Dr. Solomon who took her good arm and braced her other side by a hand on her waist.

Clementine landed on her feet with a thud. "There you see? I'm fine. It's just my arm we have to be careful of." She drew her arm in over her chest. "And that thud didn't do it any good either." She smiled broadly at Amity. "I'll be glad to get home."

Me, too, Aunt. Me, too. "Do you wish for me to order a tray or would you like to go downstairs?" Amity asked though she dreaded the answer. She needed the time to gather her wits before she saw Simon again. It shouldn't take more than one lifetime. She smiled ruefully to herself.

"Thank you, Dr. Solomon."

The doctor left, and Matilda followed after him.

Clementine placed her good arm on Amity's shoulder and together they descended the stairs one at a time. Amity spun away from the private dining parlor when she saw John Parchment and a man she'd never seen before dressed in peacock blue. Indeed, it made him look very birdlike. She'd never seen a man dressed quite like that in all her life.

"There is your Mr. Morgan over there by the window." Clementine immediately joined him.

"Mrs. Foster, good to see you feeling so much better."

"Thank you, dear boy."

Dear boy? Her stomach squeezed. It would be harder than she thought.

"Where's the diet?" A servant arrived at the table before Clementine could wonder anything else.

"Good morning, Amity. I trust you slept well?"

"Very well, thank you, Simon. And yourself?"

And this is what it would be like for the rest of their lives. His plantation was next to her father's. She would see him down through the years. See his children run and play.

"To be absolutely truthful, not very well at all."

"I hope you are feeling well, Mr. Morgan." Clementine interjected. "You know all kinds of things can befall travelers. Shall we call Dr. Solomon to attend you?"

"No, that won't be necessary."

"I heard recently of a young man who traveled to Alexandria, Lord only knows what he was exposed to, but he fell ill and nearly died."

Amity was thankful Clementine drew his attention with her stories of travel disasters. She'd no stomach for food, and the sooner they could be done, the better.

"It's a wonder you choose to travel at all, Mrs. Foster."

"Oh, that kind of thing never happens to me, dear boy. I have a tough and hearty constitution. I mean look at me, I got attacked by a bear, what just a few days ago? And here I am." She grinned quite pleased with herself.

Simon's attention was drawn to the window behind them.

"It must be time for Jax and Lucy's departure."

Amity turned toward the window.

Sure enough, the couple stood on the porch trying to get their attention.

"Departure?"

Amity tucked a nonexistent loose curl back into the knot on the top of her head. She'd been so intent on Simon she'd not told Clementine about Lucy. Embarrassment flushed her cheeks. "I'll tell you all about it after they leave, Aunt."

The day was clear and brittle. Amity scanned the road for any signs of her attackers and folded her arms against the cold.

A wagon and two horses stood in the road, filled with such supplies as were available. Lucy and Jax beamed all the good will and good feelings that two people in love setting out a new adventure could.

"I will miss you," Amity whispered as she embraced her childhood friend. "Be safe and write to me."

Lucy pulled back still holding on to Amity's shoulders.

"How will I know where you will be? Traveling all around writing your stories."

Gray certainty colored the future path in her mind. "I'll be at home. Write to me there."

"Don't forget to tell Mama I'm coming. As soon as we get the money, we'll come for her."

"I'll tell her."

Two more horses with riders stopped in front of the tavern. Mary dismounted with little Danny.

"Danny!" Clementine waved.

Mary climbed the steps of the porch. "Miss Clementine, it is good to see you out today."

Clementine placed her good hand on Mary's arm circling Danny. "Thank you for the tea." Danny reached for Clementine.

"Oh, Danny, I can't carry you right now." She placed a kiss on the top of his golden head.

Mary glanced about the porch. "It appears we are all leaving at the same time."

"Amity and I are staying for at least one more day." Clementine informed them. "Can you wait? I have something—" Clementine swung away before Mary could answer.

"Please write to us and let us know how you fair."

"I shall." Mary promised.

In the corner of her eye, Amity saw Simon hand Jax a small packet. The couple started toward the wagon. Clementine arrived on the porch with the pair of stockings she'd been knitting before her convalescence. "I was going to mail these to you, but since you are here. You might find them useful for him as you travel."

Mary's eyes filled. "They are lovely, Miss Clementine."

"Yes well, you can't have too many with a small baby." She grabbed Mary with her good arm into a rough and quick sort of half hug.

"You will write and give us your direction? And keep us appraised if you need anything."

"I will."

Danny reached up for Clementine to take him. Clementine claimed him in her good arm for all of a minute before handing him back to his mother.

Together they walked to the street. The soft mud she'd run through was now molded hard ridges. Amity put her arm through Clementine's good arm to steady her. She felt Simon's warmth at her back. She stepped up to give him more space.

When the wagon had turned at the end of the street and they could see it no more, they turned back to the tavern.

"Amity, would you care to take a walk?"

"I'm afraid I won't have time. I have to pack, and I no longer have Lucy to help me, so it will likely take all day."

"How about this evening, then?"

"Go ahead, child. I shall likely retire early leaving you all alone this evening." The conspiratorial look in Clementine's eyes was unmistakable. Amity really needed to have a talk with her.

"I'll see you later then." Simon opened the door and Amity and her aunt went back up the narrow stairs.

Amity sat across from her aunt before the fire in her aunt's room. "Aunt, I am concerned that it is not proper for me to go for an evening walk with Simon."

"For heaven's sakes, Amity, you've been out walking with him almost every night since we started this trip. What makes tonight any different?"

Amity explained what she'd seen in the corridor last night.

"Don't be so sure you know what's going on with your Mr. Morgan."

"I told you, he's not my Mr. Morgan. He is Mrs. Blackstone's."

"I'm sure there is more to this than meets the young eye."

"No. Aunt. Even if nothing happened. Mrs. Blackstone is compromised, and Simon is an honorable man. He will do the right thing. He always does. I expect that is why he wants to walk this evening." She glanced down at the thread she'd been worrying, eyes filling, "And I don't think I can stand to hear it."

"Don't be silly. Of course you can stand to hear it."

Amity looked up immediately.

"Where's your gumption, girl?"

"What?"

"Where is your spunk?"

Amity's eyes dried. "What do you mean?"

"I mean I've never known a Wright or an Archer to give up so easily."

Amity sat up straighter. "There's nothing to be done…" Though the fog that had misted through her mind began to clear.

"Isn't there? I haven't seen Mrs. Blackstone walking around declaring her engagement."

"Well, no."

"He has not asked us to wish him happy."

"No."

"Then there's time. He's asked to see you. Go and find out what he wants to say. Perhaps you've misunderstood something."

"Aunt. I know that I am an unmarried woman, but I do understand some things. One thing I do know is that I will not share my husband with anyone."

Clementine's wizened smile broke across her serious countenance. "Of course not."

23

Simon stepped into the private dining parlor to give Amity and Clementine a chance to get upstairs before heading up to his own room.

Winifred Blackstone slipped in front of him. This time fully clothed in a brown homespun gown.

Simon stepped back.

"Mr. Morgan, I'm glad I found you."

"I've got nothing to say to you."

She glanced down before approaching.

"Meekness and innocence don't work for you," Simon said.

She straightened and met his gaze head on. "I need to apologize to you for last night. It was ill conceived on my part."

Simon waited.

She took another step closer.

"That's far enough."

"Simon, I must show you something—" She stepped within the reach of his arms.

"Oh, please excuse me." Amity's soft voice entered the room before she quickly left.

"I'll talk to you later." Simon turned to follow Amity.

Mrs. Blackstone pulled on his arm. "It's a life-threatening emergency, Simon."

"What is?"

"Come with me."

"I will not go anywhere with you alone."

"Then come with us." Mr. Burns stepped into the room from the same door Mrs. Blackstone had just used.

Now he was concerned. What emergency did Mrs. Blackstone have that Mr. Burns could not handle? He needed to speak with Amity, but it could wait a few minutes while he assessed his ability to help with whatever crisis they found themselves in.

He followed them through the opposite door from the hallway and found himself in another hallway which led to another door. Through the door was suite of rooms. One of the doors was ajar.

"Mama?"

A genuine smile cracked her porcelain into softness Simon didn't think the woman possessed.

"Mr. Morgan, I would like to introduce my son, Wilfred. Wilfred, I'd like you to meet Mr. Morgan."

A boy of six or seven lay in the bed. Iron black hair like his mother. Pale like a bean plant starving for sunlight. He leaned onto his side and struggled to sit up. His mother sat down next to him and pulled him into her lap. The boy sank into his mother's embrace, too weak to sit on his own. "It's all right, sweetheart. I've asked Mr. Morgan here to help us."

His gaze shifted quickly to Mrs. Blackstone. What could he do? He was not doctor.

"Mr. Morgan has a stone that I believe will heal

you."

"What?"

"I was in contact with Tom McCabe. He found the stone for me, but when I went to retrieve it, his uncle told me that he was dead, and he'd sold the stone to you."

"You bought it." Simon stared at her, seeking truth.

"In a manner of speaking. I sent Tommy there to find the stone for me. He sent me a letter which informed me that he had found the stone and was on his way home. When he returned, he was to receive the rest of the fee I paid him."

Simon wrapped his fist around the stone. "Why didn't you just tell me that?"

"My reasons don't concern you. Suffice it to say that I have exhausted all my efforts, and this is my last resort. The stone will cure my son. Once he is better, we will leave this place and go wherever it is he desires to go."

"Do you know where you want to go, Wilfred?" Simon asked.

"Not yet."

"I don't blame you. I'm not sure I would know where I wanted to go if I had the whole world to choose from." He only knew he wanted Amity to be there wherever that was. And now it wouldn't happen because he had to give the stone to Mrs. Blackstone. "So all you need is to give him the stone?"

"Nothing is ever that simple, Simon. You should know that by now." She laid her son back on his pillow and kissed him on the head. "I'll be back to tuck you in."

"Nice to have met you, Wilfred."

"Thank you, Mr. Morgan," The boy whispered.

She closed the door behind them.

"What is the matter with him?"

"Some kind of wasting disease. Dr. Solomon has done what he can. Now it's time for something else."

Simon opened his hand the stone, clear and green rested in the center.

Mrs. Blackstone grabbed it so fast she scratched him in the process.

"What do you have to do now?"

"Follow me."

Simon's curiosity couldn't be denied. It wouldn't take long to find out just what his stone could do for the boy. In truth, he doubted it contained any supernatural properties at all though he felt it absence as acutely as though a living thing had died.

Above the kitchen, Mrs. Blackstone had created a lab of sorts. A long wooden table sat in the middle of the room. Bowls of different shapes and materials were stacked at one end with various spoons and measuring implements. A mortar and pestle occupied the center of the table.

24

After waiting an hour for Simon to arrive for their walk, Amity gave up and returned to her aunt's room to wish her good night.

"Did you enjoy your walk?" Aunt Clementine asked.

"He didn't come."

"Where is he?"

"I'm sure I don't know." Amity was perplexed.

"Did you look for him?"

Amity kept her eyes from rolling in exasperation, "Of course I looked for him. It's a tavern not an estate. I couldn't find him, and the servant I asked hadn't seen him. My father was right. If Simon Morgan was interested in me, he'd have offered for me years ago."

Clementine frowned. "I don't believe it."

"The facts are there, Aunt. He's done this to me before. It's partly why I told him we wouldn't suit."

"Explain."

"We courted when we were young. I thought I would marry him. During the summer, he'd promised me to escort me to a ball. He never came. My family and I didn't know what to make of it. I thought it odd, but I was young. We went on to the party anyway, and had a good time. The next week there was another gathering, and he did it again."

Clementine raised her eyebrows.

"I know. After the fourth time I decided that he just wasn't that interested in me after all and set about healing my heart and looking for someone else."

"But you didn't find someone."

"No, as I told you the other night, I think I've always been in love with him, and it looks as if there is no cure. Since I cannot marry a man I love, I shall have to remain single."

"It's a lonely life, spinsterhood."

"What happened to spunk?"

"My dear girl, one can't have spunk with a man who isn't there." Clementine picked up her needles and wool and began to awkwardly cast on a row. "And what will you do?"

"When I see him, I will tell him I wish that he and Mrs. Blackstone will be very happy."

"Really?"

"It is the right thing to say. I do pray he will be happy. Perhaps someday—I should not speak of Mrs. Blackstone." She kissed her aunt good night.

In the dark, under the covers in her own bed with no deep breathing in the room she knew her aunt was right. It would be a lonely life. Oh, if he'd only not kissed her, she wouldn't be able to miss the feel of his arms around her.

She sat up and lit the candle, crossed the cold floor for her writing desk. She added another log to the fire and curled up much like her aunt in a chair before the fire. She had much to tell Robertine and much more to hide in her diary.

~*~

Long after dark, the pestle still made no scratches in the smooth green stone. Wisps of hair frizzed about Mrs. Blackstone's head as she attempted to work the stone. Mr. Burns had left shortly after she struck the first blow claiming that someone must mind the tavern.

"Might I give it a try?"

"I'm not sure if it must be me in order for the magic to work."

"I am convinced the stone is not magic."

She banged the pestle down with a loud thud. "I am convinced it is, so where does that get us? Perhaps you should leave."

Perhaps he should, yes, but he couldn't. His stone lay on her table as a sacrifice for her son, and he wanted to know if his offering made a difference. "Let me try at least once, if I make a crack in it then you can finish."

She looked up at him clearly struggling with her decision.

"Look. I'm stronger than you."

She blew the hair out of her eyes and handed him the pestle. He drew the mortar across the table. The stone, his stone, lay in the bottom of the pot. Guilt surged through him. Lord, how can I break what you have made? An image of a brass snake on a pike flashed across his mind.

He brought the pestle down on the stone. The stubby club sparked and glanced off the amulet. "Do you have a sledgehammer?"

She looked from side to side. "Wait here." She placed hands on her hips.

Simon picked up the stone as soon as she left the room. He could leave now and take it with him. The hopeful face of Wilfred in his mother's arms anchored him to the room.

She returned lugging a heavy hammer. Behind her, a servant brought a heavy stone. She directed the stone be placed next to the wall and dismissed the servant to bed.

"Is it that late?" His watch confirmed it was after midnight. Sometimes he did believe the stone was magic after all. How had the time passed so quickly that he'd missed Amity again? She would forgive him once she understood what he'd been doing. He was not certain he would be given the opportunity to explain and make her understand. He'd deal with that later. The stone smoothed across his finger and thumb without a scratch. "How old is your son?"

"He will be seven in three months."

"How long has he been sick?"

"Almost eighteen months. He fell ill just after his father died."

"It must have been hard for you."

She leaned against the worktable arms crossed. "No harder than it is for anybody else."

"Give me the hammer."

Mrs. Blackstone let the handle fall toward him

without an argument. He placed his stone on the worn flat rock. His shadow blocked the light, but he still knew where it had to land. He hefted the hammer above his head at the peak of the arc the heavy weight of the hammer reversed direction and Simon added his force to the momentum. As the hammer dropped a wink of light shone along the lines of writing. Simon pulled back but couldn't stop the hammer's fall. He twisted just in time to hit the paving stone.

"Did you see that?"

"I saw you missed the stone. Give it to me."

"No. I did that deliberately."

She stuck out her hand. "Just give it to me."

"You can barely lift the thing. I can and I will do it, but first I have one request."

She crossed her arms. "No."

"I have lived with this stone for the past month, I know something about it. Please hear me out."

She moved to the work bench and repositioned her arms, eyes hard as iron shingles.

"A minister I heard once—"

"Save it." She pointed her finger at him. "I have no use for a so-called God that would take a father from a boy, and both from a wife and mother."

Give me the words, Lord. "What do you know about the stone?"

"That it has healing powers."

Simon breathed in deep. "I've done a little more research. If the stone is what I think it is, then the high priest of Israel can ask God questions."

She *hmphed*. "What good does that do?"

"Nothing, but I did attempt to ask it a question, and I think I got an answer."

"You think you did."

"It's a long story."

"Spare me."

"I think we can try to ask God if your son will be healed, but I think we need two believers to do it. Because we don't have a high priest, but Jesus said He would be in our midst if there were two of us gathered in His name."

"Well, we only have you, so give me the hammer."

"You have me." Tom Burns stepped into the room.

Simon motioned to Tom to come closer. "First I think we need to pray."

Tom agreed.

Simon held the stone open in the palm of his hand. "Father, we are gathered in the Name of the Lord Jesus." Simon opened his eyes the stone felt no different. It looked no different. "Lord, we know that we are not the high priest of Israel, but we also know that Jesus is our High Priest. Father, we ask You in Jesus' name if You will heal the boy."

A tingling ran from the stone in Simon's right hand into his heart as the stone glowed.

Tom's eyes got wide.

"We need to pray for him." Both men chimed at the same time.

Winifred stood dumbfounded.

"Freddie, get some oil from the kitchen." Tom said.

Simon nodded; he'd heard the same thing.

"With your permission, Mrs. Blackstone, I think we should go to the boy."

Mrs. Blackstone rushed out of the room. Tom followed her, and Simon followed Tom. She peeled off toward the kitchen while Simon had to run to keep up with Tom all the way back to Wilfred's room.

The fire still glowed in the boy's room. A servant slept on a narrow bed against the wall. Wilfred's breath came in shallow huffs.

Tom took the cruse of oil from Winifred's shaking hands.

Simon and Tom blessed the oil. Simon dabbed his finger in the oil and placed some on Wilfred's pale brow.

They prayed thanking God for His mercy and healing. They thanked Him for healing their unbelief. They thanked Him for His mercy in allowing them to use His Stone. They did it all in the name of the Lord Jesus. Then they stood back and waited.

Before Simon could make it to the doorjamb to lean Wilfred's eyes fluttered open.

"Mama, I think I could eat a whole elephant."

Winifred Blackstone gathered him into her arms. "Do you?" She glanced up to Tom with eyes brimming. "I don't know how to thank you."

"You don't. You thank the Lord of Heaven. He alone saved Wilfred. Didn't He, son?"

"Yes, sir, He did. I'll tell you all about it, but could I have something to eat first?"

Winifred hugged him close again. "You can have anything you want."

Simon slipped the stone into his pocket with another quiet prayer of thanks to the Lord.

The deep black of night began to lighten into blue in the window on the far side of Wilfred's bed.

"I'm going to find my bed."

"Thank you for your help."

"You are welcome." And he meant it. Eyes like sandpaper, he barely saw Amity in the early morning twilight making her way down the corridor. "Amity?"

"Simon. Are you well?"

"I am just getting to bed. I have something important to tell you, but it will have to wait until I get some sleep."

"I—"

"I really cannot talk right now." He stumbled through his door and landed on the bed.

~*~

What could she think? The irony was that it was Mrs. Blackstone herself, the night of the mob in Williamsburg, who showed her what to think. Of course, the men that night would think the worst of her, dressed as she was for a ball, mingling among a bunch of soldiers. Society's rules did have their place. The harder lesson had come with the thieves when she'd needed to walk.

Father was right. I may not understand much of the world, but at least I understand this situation. Mrs. Blackstone visited him in his room the first night. Clearly, last night was his turn to visit, and he'd not gotten any sleep.

Amity sat down with pen and ink.

Dear Simon,

As my aunt is feeling a good bit better. We believe it is time for us to begin our journey home. Mr. Moses has kindly loaned us the services of one of his hired servants to see to the wagon since Jax's happy circumstances leave us with the need of a driver. Please accept our sincere wishes for your future happiness.

Your friend,

Amity Archer

She folded the note and sealed it. His snores met her when she slipped it under the door. She let her hand stay on the door wishing she could touch him just one more time. "Good-bye, Simon" she whispered. *I will always love you.* Enough of that. Her mind fought back. "Have some spunk."

Spunk got her back to her own room before the tears fell.

~*~

He woke with the sun burning his cheek. He rolled over and felt his pocket. In the light of the sun, he could just make out a tiny scratch on the surface of the stone. The events of the night were real. He pulled himself to the edge of the bed and waited for his equilibrium to settle.

Wilfred.

Had there been a miracle?

A square of paper lay on the floor by the door. A

note?

He cracked the seal and read. What did she mean 'best wishes for his future happiness'? His happiness just took off for home without him. Trouble vibrated through his mid-section.

25

"It is a pity we did not see Mr. Morgan before we left. I have few things I should like to say to him."

They'd been in the coach about an hour. Amity didn't bother to feign interest in her writing desk. A Mrs. Peabody adventure rested on her lap unopened.

"I left him a note, so he needn't be worried."

"I care not for his worrying." Clementine worked her needles awkwardly. Her right hand functioned stiffly causing unusual clicks and taps. "I had hoped to bring you back as a bride."

"Now that I think on it, I daresay, my father had similar hopes. I, myself, had no such notion."

Clementine stopped knitting to look at her then. "Didn't you?"

"Indeed not. I hoped Simon would scare away suitors, not be one."

They laughed until Amity had to dab a tear or two from her eyes.

"You will recover, my dear."

"Yes. I know I will. I did before." The woods were thick outside their window. Amity felt for the powder pan of the shotgun lying across the seat behind her. "I will not be the same this time though."

No large animals came into view as she continued

to scan the landscape on both sides of the carriage.

They stopped less than an hour in Port Royal to change horses and eat in order to reach Tappahannock before the day was gone.

~*~

Simon approached Wilfred's room careful not to disturb the boy in case he was still sleeping.

Mrs. Blackstone still wore the same dress she'd worn throughout the night. She was curled around the boy rocking gently. One arm escaped her embrace.

Tears welled in Simon's eyes. How long had she been there?

Mr. Burns appeared at his elbow. "He finally fell asleep about an hour ago," he whispered. "Dr. Solomon has been summoned."

"What can I do?"

Winifred Blackstone gave him one of the smiles she saved for her son. "I think you've done quite enough."

"I believe you will need to get a move on if you are to reach that young lady of yours. She left at first light."

Simon spun around.

"And Mr. Morgan?"

Simon turned back.

"I will be happy to correct any misunderstandings that might have occurred. You let me know if I need to come." Mr. Burns nodded as if that would settle the issue.

Simon shook his head. He had no idea what Amity was talking about in the letter, and he did not care to figure it out. The note needed deciphering, and he doubted he could do that without speaking to the woman herself. He stopped for the footsteps behind him when he reached the main dining chamber.

"Were you aware that Mrs. Foster and her niece left early this morning?" a slightly out of breath Mr. Burns asked.

"Yes. I shall be prepared to leave in a half-hour's time."

"I shall have a meal sent to your room."

Simon acknowledged the kindness and left to prepare for his ride. He could make Port Royal quicker than the coach and wagon. He might reach them tonight. If not, surely tomorrow.

Mr. Burns brought the tray himself. "I hope you can forgive Mrs. Blackstone."

"I have nothing to forgive."

"She took your stone."

"Would you have given it freely if it were yours?"

"I'd have given my life if it would save him. Anything to save her pain. I mean—"

Simon could see that it was so. "Does Mrs. Blackstone know you feel this way?"

"That's a problem for a different day."

"Perhaps." Simon closed his satchel. "But not too long. A woman thinks you've forgotten about her if you keep her waiting too long, Burns. Don't keep her waiting."

"I've packed a meal for your trip, being you must

leave so quickly and late in the day."

Simon thanked him and sat down to eat what he could stomach before he set out on Pilgrim.

~*~

They arrived at Tappahannock close to midnight.

Amity nudged Clementine from her slumber.

A familiar, tall form rose from a chair on the porch as the coach came to a stop. He arrived at the coach just as George let down the steps. "Good evening, Aunt Clementine. Allow me."

"Field?"

"It's me."

Amity's heart swelled. "Is father all right?"

"Yes. He's entangled with Committee business, so I came."

Once Clementine was safe on the ground, he offered his hand to his sister. Amity cleared the last step before jumping into his arms. He held her close and spun her around. Five years since she'd seen him? Her closest sibling and closest friend. "Oh, Field. I'm so glad you've come. I have so many things to tell you."

"I brought Delany."

Amity's tears threatened to flow. Her family had come. How glad she was for them. Bright spots of color in a future that stretched before her alone and gray.

"Where's Simon? I heard he accompanied you."

"We left him in Fredericksburg."

A yawning Mrs. Emerson directed them to their room. Amity and her aunt would be sharing again.

Amity could not find herself sorry for the arrangement.

"Cookin's done for the day, but I could bring you a dish of coffee if you wish it." Mrs. Emerson stifled a yawn with a mittened hand.

"No, thank you, Mrs. Emerson. I hope you sleep well."

The landlady, covering her mouth with another yawn, ambled out of the room.

"Field, it's been such a long day in the coach. Do you think you could walk with me for a few minutes?"

"You are still the same." Field's tone was indulgent. "Walking in the fields and such at all hours."

"Please? It's so late and I daren't go alone."

"You? Not go alone? I don't believe it." Field laughed.

"Do credit me with some sense. It's very late, who knows what's lurking about this late at night, even in the most respectable places?"

"Go on, you two, I should like to get some sleep." Clementine shooed them off from her seat by the fireplace.

Field stepped into the room he shared with his wife and returned with his heavy coat.

Amity followed him down the stairs. She took his arm on the porch and scanned her surroundings. She didn't see anybody lurking.

"What's happened? What are you afraid of?"

They stepped off the porch and Amity began talking. As they turned the corner and made their way toward the river, she told him about being robbed. She told him about Mary and her book as they made their way back from the river toward the ordinary. She told him about Aunt Clementine and the bear as they passed the ordinary on their way to the other end of the tiny village. Field listened quietly as he always had laughing in the places he should.

"Tell me about Delany."

Field told her about his courtship and Delany's nephew as they passed the ordinary one more time. When they turned the corner and headed away from the river, he told about his wedding. "What about Simon?"

"There is nothing to say about Simon. He is in Fredericksburg. I have no idea about his plans whatever."

"Evasion does not become you. I may have been gone for five years, but I still know you better than anyone and you know more than you're letting on."

She couldn't hold the tears then. "I had hoped to unburden myself to you about that very thing, but I realize it truly is not my story to tell. Simon is your dearest friend. He will have to tell you. But I am free to say that the hope that I dared retain concerning my happiness is not to be."

"Amity. Simon is my dearest friend, barring two. Trust me when I tell you that his heart lies in one direction only and has for as long as I can remember."

The hope that would have inspired in her heart even just three days ago failed to spark. Simon would marry Winifred Blackstone, and Amity would have to live next to them for the rest of her life. "The journey must be catching up with me. I feel weary."

"Or the ten miles I think we've walked around this little village." He covered her hand with his own. "Don't lose heart, little sister. My gut tells me that this story is not done unfolding."

Their boots scraped across the wooden planking of the porch.

A horse and rider galloped into the yard. A man quickly dismounted.

Field slipped her behind his large frame before Amity could get look at him.

"Field Archer?" Simon exclaimed. "You are the absolute last person I expected to see on Emerson's porch at this time of night."

Amity stepped out from behind her brother.

"Amity," Simon breathed.

26

"Simon." Amity curtsied formally.

"It's too late at night for such nonsense." He turned to Field. "May I see Amity alone for a few minutes?"

Amity looked at her brother.

Field held both her arms at the elbow. "I'll see you in a few minutes."

Amity turned to face him. "I've been walking with my brother and so I'm cold. Will it not keep 'til the morning when we can speak in the daylight in sight of everyone?"

"Why would I want to do that?"

"For propriety's sake. I would not wish for your future wife to labor under the delusion that I have set my cap for you." Simon reached for her arms as Field had done. Amity stepped back. "Do not touch me."

He drew back.

"Amity, I have no future wife."

"You should have."

"I agree with that." And if she would stop this nonsense, he could set about providing himself with one. "Will you agree to sit with me?" He waved toward a bench attached to the porch.

"Simon."

"Please."

She sat on the farthest seat on the bench.

Simon didn't know where to begin. "Whatever happened to us, Amity?"

"What do you mean?"

"I mean, ten years ago I thought I'd found the love of my life. The next minute you told me we wouldn't suit. What happened?"

"You really don't know?"

"I was and still am bewildered."

Amity kept her gaze out on the yard. "Perhaps we haven't come as far as I thought we had, but since we are just friends, I don't suppose it will hurt to tell you, even if the only person to gain is Mrs. Blackstone."

Simon's jaw dropped.

Amity put up her hand commanding silence. "I don't know what you were thinking at the time, but I finally decided that you thought you had me all sewed up."

It was too dark to see her expression.

"Sewed up?"

"Yes. I am your best friend's sister. I was artless. You knew I was smitten. So you stopped coming around when you said you would. You stayed in your laboratory instead of escorting me as you promised. I could tell you just weren't that interested." She turned toward him. "Our friendship has deepened on this trip, and I do want you to know that I wish you every happiness in your new relationship."

"What new relationship?"

"I saw Mrs. Blackstone leave your room two

nights ago wearing almost nothing but that smile of hers."

Relief surged and he began to laugh.

She stood up before him stiff with anger. "It's not funny, Simon Morgan." She stopped shy of stomping her foot, which his sister most certainly would have done. "Last night you told me yourself you did not spend time in your room...what was I supposed to..." Her voice broke.

Simon sobered and stepped in front of her. He needed her to hear what he had to say. It was bound to be the most uncomfortable conversation he would have in all his life. Simon wiped his eyes. "You assumed we were taking turns."

Amity shook her head, clearly uncomfortable.

He couldn't blame her. "First, I need to ask you to forgive me for laughing just now. I was so relieved it just came out."

She didn't move.

"I did not dally with Mrs. Blackstone. I suppose I should be angry that you would think such a thing of me, and with such a woman." He shivered at the thought. "Though, you are not the first person who suggested something of the same to me. So I am to blame for not caring enough for appearances."

Amity softened. Her hands came out from under her arms. She clasped her hands in front of her waist.

"Mrs. Blackstone's son was dying. She came first to trick me into giving her the stone, or maybe she meant to steal it, I don't know. And last night, downstairs, in front of Mr. Burns, she asked me for it.

She took me to see her son, Wilfred."

"Did he die?"

"No. Early this morning, Tom and I prayed for him and he was healed."

"That is what you had to tell me this morning?"

"Yes."

"Tell me everything." Once again they sat on the bench, and he told her everything. Afterwards she rested her head on his shoulder. "Simon, I'm so sorry."

"I thought I couldn't lose the stone."

She pulled back; confusion ran across her face.

"I was told the stone would get me whatever I wanted most in life. I discovered you were at Millers' just after I acquired the stone. Then your father— "

"He can be a bit different."

"Yes. He asked me to escort you on this trip. That kind of thing just doesn't happen. As the trip progressed, all obstacles seemed to blow out of my way. I was so afraid I'd lose you again I was stupid."

Amity tucked back onto his shoulder.

"She tried to pulverize the stone for hours. It wouldn't break, but by then I'd already figured out how the stone is to be used. It's so God can speak to his people who would listen, like David. It's not magic. You are not here because of the stone."

"No, it wasn't the stone." She echoed and brought her palms to rest on his chest.

"Amity, I love you. I want a house full of children with brown hair that glows red in the sun and stormy blue-green eyes."

"I'm partial to hazel eyes and dark hair."

He chuckled. "We'll just have to see about that."

Simon closed the distance between them and kissed her. Amity met him with ardor of her own, matching every ounce of love and devotion he poured into their embrace.

"Simon?" Breathless she pulled back from his arms.

Breathless himself he waited for her to continue.

"Simon, I have to tell you something." She ran her hands from his shoulders to rest on his chest. "My father was right about me."

"Oh?" He placed one kiss on her hairline.

"Yes. I do wish to see the mountains."

Joyous laughter bubbled up once again from deep in his soul. "Is that right?"

"Yes."

"How soon would you like to leave?"

A Devotional Moment

A man's heart plans his way, but the Lord directs his steps. ~ Proverbs 16:9

All humans have desires of the heart—sometimes secret things we'd love to have or to accomplish. Many of us believe some of those desires are unattainable, and so we do not strive towards what we long for, and they never come to fruition. But with God, all things are possible. It's important to remember that we shouldn't discount the promptings of our hearts just because we desire something difficult or unusual. As long as we're in line with what God desires for us, with His help, we can accomplish even things that seem impossible or improbable.

In **The Dollmaker's Daughter**, the protagonist has longed for something for most of his adult life, but knowing he cannot have it, he respects God's plan for his life instead. Wrapped in faith, his world is shaken when something appears to bring about the love he has hoped for. But he finds himself questioning his own motivation and beliefs. Eventually, he comes to understand that God answers prayers, not only in His time, but when it is clear to all that He has heard all along.

Have you ever discovered that you have been gifted with something you didn't even know you wanted? Maybe you were asked to complete a task and inadvertently realized that not only did you have the talent for it, you actually enjoyed doing it, too. Maybe you were thrust into a new job and what you thought was a hardship turned out to be a blessing you never expected.

Whether it is a talent, an action, or even a person you want in your life, always remember to defer to God. The thing you want may not be for you, and the thing you never dreamed of might be your greatest blessing and joy. Hand over your wants to God. When you hand those secret longings over to Him, He may not always answer the prayer in a way you would expect, but He does answer it.

LORD, PLEASE REACH INTO THE SECRET PLACES OF MY HEART AND GIVE ME WHAT I DESIRE WITHIN YOUR WILL AND YOUR WAY. IN JESUS' NAME I PRAY, AMEN.

Thank you

We appreciate you reading this White Rose Publishing title. For other inspirational stories, please visit our on-line bookstore at www.pelicanbookgroup.com.

For questions or more information, contact us at customer@pelicanbookgroup.com.

White Rose Publishing
Where Faith is the Cornerstone of Love™
an imprint of Pelican Book Group
www.PelicanBookGroup.com

Connect with Us
www.facebook.com/Pelicanbookgroup
www.twitter.com/pelicanbookgrp

To receive news and specials, subscribe to our bulletin
http://pelink.us/bulletin

May God's glory shine through
this inspirational work of fiction.

AMDG

You Can Help!

At Pelican Book Group it is our mission to entertain readers with fiction that uplifts the Gospel. It is our privilege to spend time with you awhile as you read our stories.

We believe you can help us to bring Christ into the lives of people across the globe. And you don't have to open your wallet or even leave your house!

Here are 3 simple things you can do to help us bring illuminating fiction™ to people everywhere.

1) If you enjoyed this book, write a positive review. Post it at online retailers and websites where readers gather. And share your review with us at reviews@pelicanbookgroup.com (this does give us permission to reprint your review in whole or in part.)

2) If you enjoyed this book, recommend it to a friend in person, at a book club or on social media.

3) If you have suggestions on how we can improve or expand our selection, let us know. We value your opinion. Use the contact form on our web site or e-mail us at customer@pelicanbookgroup.com

God Can Help!

Are you in need? The Almighty can do great things for you. Holy is His Name! He has mercy in every generation. He can lift up the lowly and accomplish all things. Reach out today.

Do not fear: I am with you; do not be anxious: I am your God. I will strengthen you, I will help you, I will uphold you with my victorious right hand.
~Isaiah 41:10 (NAB)

We pray daily, and we especially pray for everyone connected to Pelican Book Group—that includes you! If you have a specific need, we welcome the opportunity to pray for you. Share your needs or praise reports at http://pelink.us/pray4us

Free eBook Offer

We're looking for booklovers like you to partner with us! Join our team of influencers today and periodically receive free eBooks!

For more information
Visit http://pelicanbookgroup.com/booklovers

How About Free Audiobooks?

We're looking for audiobook lovers, too! Partner with us as an audiobook lover and periodically receive free audiobooks!

For more information
Visit
http://pelicanbookgroup.com/booklovers/freeaudio.html

or e-mail
booklovers@pelicanbookgroup.com